KISSING MY
ASS GOODBYE

THE CLAIRE TRILOGY – BOOK THREE

TOM McCAFFREY

Black Rose Writing | Texas

ISBN: 978-1-68433-905-1 (Paperback); 978-1-68433-906-8 (Hardcover)
PUBLISHED BY BLACK ROSE WRITING
www.blackrosewriting.com

Printed in the United States of America
Suggested Retail Price (SRP) $19.95 (Paperback); $24.95 (Hardcover)
Kissing My Ass Goodbye is printed in Garamond

Cover art by Richard Lamb of Inspired Lamb Design

*As a planet-friendly publisher, Black Rose Writing does its best to eliminate unnecessary waste to
reduce paper usage and energy costs, while never compromising the reading experience. As a result, the
final word count vs. page count may not meet common expectations.

This final installment of The Claire Trilogy is dedicated to my lovely and patient wife, Lisa (né Wallen Witch), who has hung in there with me through thick and thin and never stopped believing in the young man who always wanted to be a writer. I love you forever.

KISSING MY
ASS GOODBYE

PROLOGUE
(NEVER SAW IT COMING)

Merry Christmas!

Two years into the federal Witness Protection Program (WITSEC) had changed my life beyond anyone's dreams. As Jimmy McCarthy, one time mafia lawyer, I died figuratively the day I testified as the key trial witness in the federal district court for the Southern District of New York in a R.I.C.O. case against my mafia boss, Ty Valachi, and his associates. As Jimmy Moran, the gentleman rural day-trader, I died literally later that same year when those mafia family members tracked me down to my isolated homestead in the northern reaches of Colorado and put a bullet through my human heart. As Jimmy Moran 2.0, the Tellurian-Centaurian hybrid, I felt like I was about to die again.

"What do you mean, we're pregnant?"

01001010 01110101 01110011 01110100 00100000 01110111
01101000 01100001 01110100 00100000 01001001 00100000
01110011 01100001 01101001 01100100 00101100 00100000
01110111 01100101 00100111 01110010 01100101 00100000
01110000 01110010 01100101 01100111 01101110 01100001
01101110 01110100 00100001

Just what I said, we're pregnant!

My wife, Gina Moran 2.0, teleported from the rocker in the far corner of our bedroom to right beside me in the bed and waved the pen shaped object before my eyes with such speed it remained a blur until I snatched it from her hand and could see the Clearblue blue-tipped applicator with the word *Pregnant* on its tiny screen.

Atta boy, Jimmy! Let me be the first to congratulate the happy couple. The sound of Claire the Mule's husky feminine voice popping into my head totally uninvited only added to my confusion. The moment I blocked her I heard her indignant bray immediately followed by the external sound of that same husky voice shouting "you suck Jimmy!" from the paddock on the side of the house. One unexpected blessing from the physical isolation of our property was that my closest neighbors were too far away for any sound to carry, unless the wind was there to help it along. This hypothesis had been proven multiple times over the past few years, including muting the sound of multiple gun shots, as long as you were using the appropriate silencers. Silencers are golden.

Of course, I was immediately reminded that distance was no barrier for telepathic communication when the tall blond beauty, the Centaurian, Michelle 5.0, who, with her husband, Everett, were our closest neighbors in Berthoud, Colorado, appeared sitting on the edge of our bed, snatched the small blue wand from my hand and glanced at its tiny screen before I had a moment to object.

"Holy shit! You are pregnant!" The sound of Michelle's voice had barely registered before the two women disappeared from the bed and were engaged in a full-blown bear hug by the doorway of our bedroom. The intensity of these two powerful beings hopping with joy was such that the clock on the far wall started to shake from the transferred vibration. I could not help but notice that, despite having no close familial relation, Gina's recent genetic hybridization now caused her to look like a dark-haired, slightly younger, and equally beautiful version of her adopted Centaurian sister. Gina was actually glowing.

"Is this even possible?" I shouted to get their attention.

Given that, despite our recent genetic evolution, we were both in our mid-sixties in human years, and that Gina and I were never able to become pregnant during the forty-plus human years we had been married, and it was not for lack of trying, I thought this was a fair question.

"Oh, she's pregnant all right," Michelle called over to me. "I can feel the energy of the new life within her."

Michelle held Gina at arms-length and focused her stare at my wife's abdomen.

"Spoiler alert, it's a boy!"

CHAPTER ONE
(RETURN OF CHRISTMAS MAGIC)

Given the special holiday, Gina had planned an open house for every human and mystical member of our crew to celebrate our blended family. Over the past two years each of the adult members had laid everything on the line using their natural and supernatural talents to protect the group and each other. Using our respective talents, Lenny, Everett, Michelle, Helen, Bobbi, Eddie, Gina, and I successfully vanquished a mafia hit team that had come to our new homestead seeking reprisal. Afterword, Michelle's extraterrestrial mate, Everett, and I had defended the choices we made, during the heat of battle that bloody night, on the far side of our galaxy. Even our newest adult acquisition, Whitey, had recently used his unforseen gifts to protect the family from some of earth's more natural predators.

Two of the younger members of the group, the barely adult sisters, Scarlett and Savanna, had made their contributions years before while they were just children, when, out of their abundance of love, they taught the equally young mule foal, Claire, how to vocally capitalize on her mythic genetic mutation. The remaining child of our group, Lucian, one of Claire's earliest confidants, generously shared the ranching skills he had been taught as the youngest child of his own rural family, no questions asked.

And we had buried Mister Rogers, Claire's true love.

This family of discarded parts had been thrown together and assembled on the fly without instructions, and then forged in fire. It was now miraculously growing organically from within, and it was time to celebrate this season of giving.

During my past life as the fallible mafia lawyer Jimmy McCarthy, before my more recent life as the fallibly human Jimmy Moran, I had always resisted the urge to decorate for the Christmas holiday. Gina and I never really entertained at home and there were no children in the house to enjoy the magic of the season. Back in New York, once my sister disappeared across the pond and the McCarthy brothers drifted apart, our only festive nod to Christmas was attending Ty Valachi's black-tie Christmas eve bash, along with hundreds of his closest friends and "family." All who attended were showered with the best food and entertainment the mafia kingpin's illicit money could buy. But try as he might, Ty could not buy the magic that made the season special, given that his faux generosity was paid for over the course of the year through the blood and misery of others. But that never kept me from accepting the litigation bag full of Benjamins Ty gave me as my annual Christmas bonus, which helped to seed my overseas accounts which the feds never found, and which continued to propagate my family's wealth, even after Gina and I entered the Witness Protection Program.

Gina had spent a healthy chunk of that money this year buying expensive, though tasteful, presents for everyone, including the dogs, Maeve and Blue, and of course, Claire. Gina was giddy with excitement this year as Christmas day grew nearer, although some of that lightheadedness could have been brought about by her own recent transformation into a Tellurian-Centaurian hybrid.

My wife's festive intensity was completely understandable. I had missed our first Christmas in Berthoud because I was off travelling through space to argue the last and most important case in my ever-expanding lifetime, human and otherwise, before the High Council of my newly acquired ancestors on Proxima Centauri b. Given that it turned out to be my own capital case, it was great to go out on a win.

While our second Christmas found our blended family back together as a group, it remained understandably subdued due to the recent loss of Mister Rogers, and the unexpected difficulties imposed upon Gina and my personal relationship by the law of unintended consequences. Those difficulties tested the mettle of this family to its breaking point, but with the intercession of the group, and the alien impulsiveness of Michelle, we survived it, and we were now the stronger for it.

In an effort to put the past truly behind us, Gina had gone overboard this year decorating the house, both inside and out, in a winter wonderland motif. Working at Centaurian speed, it was effortlessly completed in one night, including stringing a hundred yards of chaser, outdoor colored lights along all three rails of the entire front fence line. There was plenty of time to do everything when you can move with the speed of thought and no longer needed to sleep, both added benefits of our genetic transformations. The overnight snow had blanketed the earth with a powdery confection that glistened like diamonds as we sipped our coffee and watched the sun rise over our handiwork along the front of our property.

The exploding flurry of white powder suddenly rising before us heralded the return of Michelle with her Centaurian mate, Everett. The couple appeared momentarily on our front porch, before clasping hands and teleporting directly into the kitchen behind us. Everett's immediate attempt to coax a cup of coffee from my Keurig, was stymied by Michele's insistence that he complete his mission to congratulate us both on the good news. But before he could get a word out, Michelle had shrieked in her own joy, clasped Gina in another bear hug and the two disappeared. We could hear their laughter coming from the upstairs bedroom.

"Merry Christmas and congratulations." Everett deadpanned as he patted me on the shoulder before returning to the Keurig and his mission of choice, imbibing earthly caffeine. There was still a sprinkle of snow covering his Centaurian thick blond mane.

After our victorious return from Centauri, Everett and Michele relinquished the nondescript human forms they maintained throughout their decades on earth for their comparably upgraded Centaurian visages. They looked like a couple of tall, beautiful, middle-aged Norwegians who could still compete on their country's Olympic swim team. Of course, with a little stylish prodding from Gina, they now wore their hair and dressed in a fashion that would have looked equally at home on the cover of Glamour magazine. Their flawless translucent skin added to their youthful appearance. Despite my own post-Lazarus transformation, which gave me the body of a middle-aged triathlete, I rejected any and all of Gina's attempts to convert me from denim to cashmere. I still rocked my now thick brown hair tied off in a ponytail, with a few inches of neatly maintained beard covering my jawline.

"Michelle tells me it's a boy." Everett continued.

I appreciated Everett's attempt to engage me in old-fashioned, human dialogue, as opposed to the far more expeditious exchange of information telepathically through the binary code I had come to master since my return from space. This was the first time discussing such an emotional moment in my life with anyone other than Gina, and I would have felt cheated had it been shared solely through sterile numbers.

"Have you mentioned it to the others?" I asked.

Whoops. Was that supposed to be a secret? Claire interjected telepathically to both of us.

Despite my rapid evolutionary advancement, I still had not gotten completely used to the idea that a number of the other more practiced members of our group could freely access my mind unless I purposely blocked them. But just like putting down the toilet seat, it still was more an exception to my conscious practices than the rule.

"Oh my God – Oh my God – Oh my God!" Now it was Bobbi's bubbly voice chiming in from the ether. *"We're going to have a baby! Oh, and he's a special boy."*

"Congrats Jimmy!" Whitey's feral voice joined our mental party line. Everett laughed.

"We'll talk about this more later when you all get here." I mentally messaged, *"But until then can you all just stay out of my head?!"*

"Sure thing," responded Claire. I could feel the others had already disconnected.

"You too," I countered.

"Suit yourself," Claire responded, before slipping into that husky, Lurchy laugh, *"See you later with the others under the back deck. Aunty Claire out!"* Thank God, Claire could not hold a microphone, or she would have dropped it.

Once he was certain that we were completely alone, Everett continued speaking, with a surprisingly considerate tone to his voice.

"Given all that we've been through together, and please excuse the pun, this is the first time I've ever sensed you were rattled."

"Well, given the circumstances," I responded, ignoring Everett's poor attempt at baby humor, "this is a bit out of my wheel-house."

"Are you kidding?" Everett continued rhetorically. "There is not a problem in our Universe that can stump Jimmy Moran!"

"Really," I replied, "then how come I can't figure out how Gina got pregnant in the first place."

"I can only assume it was the old-fashioned way." Everett said, then chuckled.

My trip to Proxima Centauri b the year before had shown me that comedy did not come naturally to the Centaurians, although the cute little Doctor Nim, who treated me like an adorable lab rat, did demonstrate an inherent sense of bawdy humor. Eighty years on earth had not moved Everett's comedy needle very far, but I gave him credit for trying.

"Seriously," I continued, "Gina couldn't get pregnant as a healthy young human. And I thought Centaurian women needed some special enzyme to turn on their baby oven?"

Everett gave that some thought.

"Well," he posited, "as to the latter, from what I could glean during our trial before the High Council, you guys are hybrids, so I can't be sure what genetic switches were thrown when you were zapped by the Hadron Distributor. And you retained a lot of junk genes we don't have."

He continued to ruminate while he slowly fixed himself another cup of coffee. It took all of my patience to keep myself from peeking into his mind.

"And as for the former," he finally added, "did you ever think that it was you shooting blanks when you were just a human?"

Despite the fact that I had always considered that as a back-burner possibility, it stung just a little to hear it verbalized by another male. I guess I should have evolved more as a human before evolving into a Centauri.

"So, maybe Gina doesn't need the enzyme booster and your zapping repaired your plumbing," Everett added.

At that moment, Michelle reappeared with Gina. I could hear Blue following their scent down the stairs from the Tower. I wondered what the dogs made of our new way of moving around the house.

"Enough of your locker-room banter, gentlemen," Michelle quipped, "Gina needs us to pick up some extra fruits and vegetables at Walmart."

"And we need to go outside and discuss everything with Claire before the others arrive," Gina added, pointing at me.

Michelle gave Gina a final hug and placed her hand on Gina's still taut belly. She closed her eyes and slowly sucked in a deep breath.

"He's beautiful." Michelle whispered, before snatching Everett's hand and disappearing.

It was clear that being able to sense my still zygotic offspring was one more Centaurian trick I had not yet mastered. I hoped it would not take me my five century Centaurian lifetime to figure it all out. I received one more reminder that the males of any species were always a step behind their female counterparts, when a moment later, Gina grabbed my hand and we found ourselves transported to Claire's Lair.

CHAPTER TWO
(SHARING THE WEALTH)

The small barn was empty, and we could see Claire's fresh tracks in the snow leading around the back of the barn and out of the side paddock. Gina scanned the area, grabbed my hand and a moment later we were standing beside Mister Rogers' graveside, which lay right behind the bat house in the large open area of our back property we call the soccer field.

Claire was a few yards away nuzzling the neck and mane of the glowing, holographic version of her dead mate, so we remained a respectful distance apart for a moment until she sensed our presence. I distracted myself by studying the frozen pond in the distance beyond. The hologram suddenly disappeared, and Claire turned in our direction.

"Sweetie!" Claire shouted to Gina, "C'mere and let this old mare give Mommy some sugar!"

I did not see Gina move. She appeared directly in front of Claire, wrapped her arms around the mule's neck and buried her face beneath her jawline. I could not tell who was controlling the movement, but the two rocked from a central pivot, side-to-side like a giant metronome. Gina was whispering something unintelligible. They were both sobbing.

"Musha, musha, musha . . ." Claire whispered a line my mother used to employ whenever she needed to comfort someone, often me, up close and personal. "It's all going to be alright."

I felt a bit confused by the mixture of emotions I was sensing and tried to reach into both of their minds but found myself blocked.

"Let's get out of the snow and go back to the barn –" before Claire had completed her thought, Gina had whisked them both away, leaving only a small snow dervish in their wake. Before I could follow, Claire's husky voice popped into my head.

Why don't you go back to the house and grab yourself another cup of coffee, Jimmy, and let us women share a special moment.

I could not understand what was happening, but my experience in Colorado had taught me that there were times, like this, where it was useless to resist the flow. I had to consciously choose to walk human style the long way back to the house along the western property line to make sure I gave the two closest females in my life plenty of space.

Still moving at human speed, I busied myself setting up the back patio space with the oversized barn table and chairs we used for our full family gatherings. Blue lay sleeping beneath one of the two industrial sized heaters found on either end of the area which maintained a temperate zone that allowed the large stone fountain over by the winter dormant, ivy-covered retaining wall to continue to flow even during the coldest weather.

I fixed myself that suggested cup of coffee in the basement kitchenette that opened through sliding doors onto this under-space, then sat down at the Jesus spot in the middle of the table and let my mind drift free along with the gurgling sound of the fountain. I remembered the line from John Milton's poem, "On His Blindness,"

they also serve who only stand and wait.

Lost in thought, I ignored the fluttering sounds of moth-like wings circling my head until I lifted the cup to my lips and spotted three tiny, translucent faces peaking over the cup's far side, each resting between three pairs of correspondingly tiny hands. Having gotten my attention, with mouse-like squeaks, these three English Sprites that my sister Bonnie and her spouse, Tessa, had delivered during their Thanksgiving visit a year ago, the day of Gina's evolution, now propelled themselves into a synchronized back flip and hovered in the air before me.

My sister, Bonnie McCarthy, had been estranged from our family for decades while she pursued her successful life in England as a progressive, openly gay Headmistress of an elite British school, where she also met and married the love of her life, Tessa De Mille, a British baroness from the House of Tudor. We had reunited the year before, after all four of her brothers had been murdered by the mafia and I had been miraculously resurrected in my present, genetically modified state, by the Centaurians, Everett and Michelle.

And it turned out that Bonnie's lesbian closet also contained her birthright as our family's Seanchaí, the custodian of our Clan's oral history, and her anointment by our maternal grandmother as the protector of Daoine Sidhe, the last of the Tuatha De Danann, or, as we Yanks like to call them, the Fae. Bonnie's magic, including her own telepathic abilities, had been handed down through the family's female bloodline from time immemorial. When Nana Burke crossed the veil, she passed her mystical baton to the eldest female worthy of her powers. Bonnie fit the bill.

The "fairy godmothers," as I liked to call them, had stayed with us for ten days over the recent Thanksgiving holiday, a non-event back in England, so they remained across the pond and were hosting a group of Tessa's close "Ox-Bridge" friends over the Christmas holiday at their magical country estate in Salisbury.

I have always been terrible remembering simple human names, so remembering the names for the three Sprites, Alieki, Brentisa, and Cirrha, was out of the question. They were immediately relegated to the acronym ABC, and quickly adapted to responding accordingly. And while I had failed to master the chirping Sprite dialect, they understood English perfectly, these particular three having graced the British countryside since before Chaucer wrote his opening line of the Canterbury Tales, *"Whan that Aprill with his shoures soote,"* in Middle-English. They looked great for their age.

"Okay," I said, placing the coffee cup down on the table and extending my open palm, "I have a very important message for you to carry to Bonnie and Tessa."

The three Sprites flitted in a synchronized summersault over the edge of the coffee cup and onto my open palm, where they alighted with the gentleness of a wary fly.

I removed my iPhone with the other hand and held it out for them to see.

My Sprites were very familiar with our cell phones, having made a continuing game out of the quick-draw attempts to capture them on camera, by our close friend, and resident U.S. Marshal and bodyguard, Mark "Lenny" Lenahan. Even with his self-proclaimed "Sundance Kid" hand speed, that he had used to effectively protect this family that bloody night of the Storm two years earlier, their images always appeared as tiny glowing blurs on the edges of his digital screen. I had never made the attempt using my now Centaurian speed, but the Sprites must have assumed I was about to try, because they began to hover above my palm in anticipation of another round of photo-tag.

When I realized what was occurring, I placed the phone on the table.

"No, ABC, I was going to use this," giving the prone cell phone a tap for emphasis, "to give Bonnie and T this news, but given how truly special it is, I want you to carry it to them."

The disappointment on their faces at the loss of a game quickly morphed into anticipation as they all alighted on my palm and sat, cross-legged, like a group of captivated toddlers.

"Now that I have your undivided attention, I need you to return to England and tell Bonnie and T that –"

I felt the rush of wind and then powerful arms encircling my shoulders.

"–We're pregnant!" shouted Gina.

The Sprites certainly understood that news, as they all simultaneously launched into the air and linked hands in a rotating circle like free-falling skydivers, chirping excitedly to each other before disappearing, in between blinks, into the ether.

CHAPTER THREE
(THE NOTHING LEFT TO REVEAL PARTY)

Despite her having stolen my thunder with the Sprites, I was happy to see Gina's excitement return. Other than some residual redness around her eyes, there was no sign of the emotion she had displayed out on the back field before disappearing with Claire. I was about to broach the subject, when I heard Claire throwing the bolt on the side gate to her paddock. I could hear the sounds of her hooves against the packed snow over the winter hardened soil as she trotted over to the patio.

Gina gazed into my eyes while rifling through my mind and whispered, "silly hormones! Claire sorted me out." She winked and gave me a quick peck.

"Lenny is on route with Maeve," Claire huskily half-whinnied as she entered the patio. "They are stopping to pick up Bobbi, Helen and Eddie on their way."

"I better get started on brunch," Gina said before giving me another quick hug and disappearing.

I telepathically reached out to Michelle and Everett and accidently caught them *in flagrante delicto* for a split-second before they realized they had an audience and blocked me. *Just like rabbits. Merry Christmas indeed!*

"Eww, eww, eww!" Claire bellowed as she spun in circles behind me. "I'm never going to get that image out of my head!"

When was I going to learn to put the toilet seat down?

"That's what you get for snooping in my brain uninvited," I said, laughing.

I guess Michelle was right when she told me back in the day that they were similar enough to us to make it fun. I felt a sudden flush of embarrassment rise up my neckline and onto my cheeks. It was like catching your parents "at it."

A sudden feral howl could be heard in the distance from the direction of the front property, and Blue leapt to her feet and rushed off in its direction.

A moment later Blue returned followed by the oversized human form of Whitey Fronsdahl, carrying an equally oversized load of Christmas-wrapped presents in his muscular arms.

"For the youngsters!" Whitey declared, holding the packages out for inspection.

With his luminescent white locks and beard, it was not hard to imagine Whitey playing the role of St. Nick, although he would need to put on quite a few pounds on his power-lifter build.

One of the boxes for the presents was long and sleek.

Whitey noticed my observation and responded telepathically, *What? It's for Lucian. He is ten now, old enough for his own Ruger 10/22, and I promised him I would take him shooting at Lenny's firing range.*

Scarlett, Savanna and Lucian were spending Christmas with their respective blood families but were going to come by on Boxing Day for a meal with their family of misfits. Gina could not wait to spoil them with the truck load of presents she had been hiding in the basement storage area. Thank God, they each remained completely human, so we only had to prevent their figuring things out using their five senses. Our resident psychic-witch, Bobbi Angelini, had promised the two young ladies, both college students in their twenties, to teach them the craft whenever they were ready. But I was happy they had thus far declined. The three youngsters were my last bastion of normalcy in my relatively new paranormal existence.

Blue's ears perked up and she flew out from beneath the table and around the side of the house. I heard car doors slamming and the unmistakable voice of Lenny shouting "Go get her, Maeve!"

Moments later, black and white fur blurs rocketed around the back corner of the house and then slipped out through the side gate that Claire had left open to her paddock. I visually followed their paths through the snow out beyond Mr. Rogers' gravesite before being distracted by the cluster of humans turning the corner into our backyard.

Leading the pack was the tall and sinewy Mark "Lenny" Lenahan. He was wearing his best pair of blue jeans, Lucchese Roper Riding Boots, a smart blue blazer over a starched white man-tailored shirt. A navy-blue wool cap with the words U.S. Marshal stenciled in white around a star above its peak, rested on his now lengthy greying mane. Completing his ensemble were two blue boxes containing Macallan scotch; Single Malt, 12 Year Double Cask.

Directly behind Lenny appeared Helen La Lousis, the Greek proprietress of Hygiene's most famous eatery, the Oracle of Pythia. She was dressed in a personally tailored, navy colored, Emily Meyer suit, with a cashmere pink scarf loosely tied around her neck, donning her own pair of Lucchese boots, and wearing her thick blond hair cut close and away from her androgynous face, which had just the hint of primer. Matching single carat solitaires, glistening in the winter sun, graced each of her olive toned ear lobes. She was carrying a large bottle of *Idoniko Tsipouro*, a Greek liqueur.

Beside Helen floated Bobbi Angelini, our resident psychic-witch, dressed in a draping, form fitting black knitted gown whose extended hemline brushed gently along the top of the snow. The alabaster skin of her exposed face matched the winter powder in purity and brightness, and was smartly accented by just enough rouge, mascara, and eye liner to identify her as the more feminine of the couple. Her jet-black hair cascaded over her shoulders, which were wrapped in a long, onyx colored cashmere stole. Bobbi's right arm was entwined in tandem with Helen's left.

Following up the rear appeared the slight but fit form of Eddie Angelini, ex-army Ranger and Bobbi's older brother, who now lived with Bobbi and Helen and worked as the head chef at the Oracle. Eddie was dressed in comparable Cowboy chic to Lenny's ensemble, but the finery of his haberdashery was offset by his long, wispy, and unkempt beard. I could detect the delicious aroma of various Greek pastries wafting from the large wicker basket he carried on his right shoulder, causing that sleeve of his jacket to slide down just enough to expose the edge of his battle earned tattoo. Eddie set the basket on the closest end of the table, went right over to Claire, and wrapped his wiry arms around her neck. Then he reached into his jacket pocket and withdrew a small plastic bag that contained a cylindrical green treat.

"Oooh, Dolmathakia," Claire cooed. "You sure know how to win a girl over."

"Speak of the Devil and he appears!" Lenny shouted as he stomped the snow off his boots and proceeded to his now usual spot at the opposite end of the table, right across from Whitey. Both men were so tall that they easily performed the double-tap, fist-pat embrace across the width of the tabletop, causing Lenny's jacket to ride up and expose the imprint of his lethal Glock 45 on his right hip. Lenny handed Whitey one of the boxes and cheered "You can do the honors my Lycanthropic brother from another mother."

Bobbi disengaged from Helen's arm and drifted right through the sliding glass doors, mentally proclaiming her pursuit of the *mother-to-be*. Helen came over to me and, liqueur bottle in hand, engaged me with a hug that would have cracked the ribs of my human form. She nestled her head on my shoulder and whispered naughtily, "If there was ever a male body that could make me switch teams, yours might be it." I am absolutely certain I blushed.

Lenny guffawed when Helen then slapped me hard on the ass with her free hand and shouted "Merry Christmas! Now that's what I'm talking about."

My facial flush barely had time to fade before returning full-on with the spontaneous appearances of Michelle and Everett, dressed in matching sexy Santa and Mrs. Claus outfits. Everett immediately began teasing Lenny by extending his hand to shake then disappearing each time Lenny reached for it.

"Never pegged you for a voyeur, Jimmy," Michelle hissed suggestively, while wagging her finger in my direction. "We'll have to learn to keep our mental blinds closed from now on when we are doing the dirty!"

Claire responded with another round of husky voiced, "Ew, ew, ew," as the momentary clip from their alien sex-tape involuntarily replayed in my head while my skin did its best Chameleon impression to match the red in Michelle's Christmas outfit.

"Don't need to read your mind to know that whatever it was, it must have been epic," Helen cackled.

"Always is," Michelle retorted, winking at the now blushing Everett.

At that moment, Bobbi reappeared at the sliding doors and proclaimed, "Charter Members of the Misfit Moran Family, I give you our latest Christmas miracle!"

As Bobbi slipped deliberately out of the way, Gina appeared, literally glowing, with a notable baby bump replacing the taut, athletic belly from hours before. My jaw dropped.

"Oh," Michelle said matter-of-factly as she glanced down at the bump, "in this morning's excitement, I must have forgotten to mention that the gestation period on Centauri is only three human months. Merry Christmas!"

CHAPTER FOUR
(TOASTS OVER TOAST)

Why was I the only one who showed the least bit of worry at the situation we now found ourselves in?

To everyone else, this was just one more adventure. It was as if this relatively uneventful year following Gina's genetic evolution created a vacuum that required an adrenaline antidote.

The females, including Claire, all huddled around Gina by the doorway exchanging excited comments of anticipation while at the far end of the table Lenny opened the Macallan and poured ample shots for everyone in the breakfast juice glasses that Eddie had brought out from the kitchenette. Lenny's first attempt to propose a toast appeared to fall on deaf ears among the excited crowd, so he downed his glass, poured himself another two fingers worth of single malt, removed his boot and banged it on the table like a gavel.

"Members of this illustrious body, I would like to propose a toast." He bellowed.

Whitey ushered the resisting women over to their places at the table and began to distribute glasses to every present member of the party, withdrawing the last amber filled glass from Gina's reach and replacing it with one filled with healthy orange juice poured by Eddie. Everett disappeared and returned with a large bowl of water for Claire. He did not spill a drop. Maeve and Blue sought out their usual spots beneath the table and curled up to rest.

Claire looked over at Lenny.

"Mr. Lenahan," she said melodramatically, followed by an interesting mule curtsy, "you have the floor." Lenny bowed his head respectfully in Claire's direction, and, still holding his boot in one hand, his glass in the other, addressed the group:

"Over these past two years I have watched our rag-tag family of talented misfits grow through random acquisition." Lenny took a moment to put back on his boot, then continued. "The right person –"

Claire loudly cleared her throat with a husky "Ahem," and Lenny pivoted effortlessly.

" – the right *creature* – seemed to come along at just the right time to serve the greater good." Lenny stopped for a moment and looked over at Claire for approval. She nodded.

"Proceed."

"All of us have been tested to our limits and each has come through for this family. I am forever grateful to be one of us. And while Jimmy and Gina reject any suggestion that they are the head of this family, they certainly are its heart."

I glanced over at Gina and could see that her eyes matched mine tear for tear.

"Hear, hear!" Whitey interjected playfully and gave me an affectionate pat on the shoulder that almost made me drop my glass. Lenny continued.

"Now our fellowship is expanding one more time, from within. While this event may not be *natural* in the truest sense of that word, given what we have all experienced as a family, I find that the concept of *natural* is highly overrated. However, what does seem *organic*, is that our newest member comes from our family's heart. Jimmy and Gina, so we welcome the upcoming birth of your child as our child. I know I speak for all of us when I say that it will be showered with all our love and protected by all of our gifts, as long as we draw breath."

" – and beyond," Bobbi chimed.

Lenny tossed back his shot, and the rest of the group followed suit, while Claire stomped repeatedly on the concrete patio as she drank from her bowl, which caused the cutlery to dance around the table. Everett suddenly appeared beside Lenny, threw his arm across the back of his shoulders, and gave him a powerful squeeze that pulled Lenny off balance.

"Who would have thought that this human could be so eloquent!" Everett exclaimed while he righted his friend safely back on his two feet, drawing laughter from the rest of the group and causing Lenny to blush, just a little.

"Thank you Lenny," Gina responded, extending her half-filled juice glass in toast to him, before repeating that motion to each individual member of the group along the table edge. "And thank you all for being here with us, and for all that you are, and for all that you do. Merry Christmas!"

Gina concluded by leaning over and giving me a three Mississippi kiss, while the others responded in applause.

"Now let's eat," Eddie said, leading Helen back into the kitchenette and reappearing moments later with ample platters of breakfast meats and sides, which Michele instantaneously distributed among the plates at the table.

As I watched them all dig into their breakfast, listening to their happy banter, and appreciating the miracles that had brought us all together, my lawyer brain kept niggling at me, so I closed my mind to any access by the others. This family was embarking one more time into unchartered territory, with no instruction book. And while our collective and ever-expanding gifts had performed amazing feats, including resurrecting me, none of us had dealt with the miracle of the creation of life, human or otherwise, from scratch.

And what was I to make of Petrichor's recent, pre-conscious message? How could it be true? For the moment, I buried it as deep in my mental vault as I could find, back among my mafia memories, and made sure I put the toilet seat down, before returning my attention to the love before me.

CHAPTER FIVE
(MIDWIFE IN THE HOUSE)

"You are going to need a midwife!"

Bobbi's post-breakfast declaration brought the attention of the company back to the issue at hand.

"Well, you certainly won't be able to stroll into a local Gynecologist's office," chimed in Lenny, as he wiped the traces of his sausages and eggs off his moustache, "unless you want Uncle Sam to be delivering that child somewhere in the subterranean bowels of Area 51."

The harsh but obvious truth to Lenny's statement ladled another thick layer of apprehension on top of the fear I was already trying to stifle just over the idea of two, sixty-plus, Tellurian-Centaurian hybrids having a baby at an accelerated rate. The innumerable dangers associated with this pregnancy made the original fear of reprisal from the Valachi family that drove us into WITSEC in the first place, look like a walk in the park. My "lawyer" brain quickly assessed the who, what, where and why of our present situation, but was struggling with the "how." Gina's nursing background would certainly be useful, but she was not about to deliver her own baby. *Fool for a client.*

"I gotta guy!" Helen exclaimed. "I mean, she's a gal."

"That's right!" Bobbi excitedly continued her paramour's intercepted thought, "Eileen Cotto used to be a fully licensed midwife in California, before leaving behind 'those screeching breeders,' as she liked to call them. She changed careers and got her DVM at CSU. She refers to herself as a 'mid-life retread.' Set up practice in Longmont a few years ago and never looked back."

"She's one of our Sappho Sisters," Helen explained with a hint of pride. "She knows how to keep a secret."

"Sappho? DVM? CSU?" Lenny retorted. "WTF?"

But the rest of the crew were already telepathically sharing Bobbi's retrieved images. Eileen appeared as an attractive, well-turned-out, middle-aged woman with silver-blond hair, sitting around one of the private tables in Helen's restaurant, The Oracle, regaling the attending circle of dominant women with her latest midnight adventure extracting a breech calf from her uncooperative mother.

"And the old dear never complained once during the four-hour delivery," Eileen said, "not even when I had to shove her prolapsed uterus back into place and give her a couple of staples. The whole thing reminded me of the time one of my California breeders needed an episiotomy . . ."

Given that Bobbi had gotten into Eileen's mind to provide a bird's-eye view of her story, I tuned out of the image just in time to listen to the other gifted members at our table, including Gina, erupt into laughter at the memory of Eileen's recounted punchline.

"What did I miss?" Shouted Lenny, obviously disappointed.

"Don't ask," Helen responded, "this is 'Bobbi sharing' that we're talking about."

"Trust me," I consoled him, "speaking as a male, whatever it was, it would put you off the female form forever."

"Wasn't that bad," Whitey countered. "Seen far worse as a wolf."

"I thought it was fascinating," Everett affirmed. "And that Eileen sure knows how to spin a tale. Story, not wag."

"Well, I'm not having my son delivered by a vet!" I declared in my most officious voice, hoping I had put the matter to rest.

"Hold on a second," Claire interjected defensively, "I'll take a vet over some diva doctor any day. They show up, day or night, weather and T-times be damned."

"In the end, it's not your call, Jimmy" Gina quickly countered in her best and final countermand. "Based on my own professional experience as an RN, Eileen's hilarious anecdote demonstrated that she knows how to deliver a baby during the most trying of circumstances. She's no quitter."

"And, given some of her other stories shared after a bottle of Ouzo," Helen offered with a smile. "Eileen certainly knows her way around the female bits and pieces."

"Bring her by." Gina declared, putting the matter to rest.

"Sooner rather than later," Michelle added while glancing imperceptibly at Gina's belly, her own mind literally masking her concern.

"Cheer up, Jimmy." Lenahan offered consolingly. "To torture one of my favorite sayings – In the land of the blind, the one-eyed Lady is Queen! Seems like Eileen is the only game in town."

CHAPTER SIX
(First Time For Everything)

"She thinks she's coming to assess Claire." Bobbi explained to the group that had gathered again at our home for brunch on Boxing Day so the adults could watch the younger crew open their presents. The older girls and Lucian had just left in their jeep, loaded with their Christmas swag. However, Lucian's Ruger 10/22 was left behind in Whitey's protective hands.

Gina had worn a looser outfit so she would not accidently share the news before she was ready.

"Let me ease her into a discussion about the midwifing once we've had a chance to feel her out." Bobbi continued.

Since it was a Saturday, Eileen promised Bobbi to swing by as a favor after she completed an emergency surgery she was performing to remove Christmas tinsel from the bloated belly of a five-year old's lop-eared rabbit.

"Fine," Claire responded. "But no blood tests and no shots!"

I had been doing a little on-line research on human pregnancy and was worried to learn that the baby bump that seemed to appear literally overnight, would have placed Gina at the end of her first trimester. Based on the Centaurian timeline, that only gave me about sixty-days to get my head around whatever was coming.

"Stop worrying," Bobbi admonished me in front of the rest of the crowd at the table. "I've seen what is coming and the baby is going to be perfect, and then some."

01001001 01100110 00100000 01111001 01101111 01110101
00100000 01100100 01101111 01101110 00011001 01110100
00100000 01100010 01100101 01101100 01101001 01100101
01110110 01100101 00100000 01101101 01100101 00101100
00100000 01110100 01100001 01101011 01100101 00100000
01100001 00100000 01101100 01101111 01101111 01101011
00101110
If you don't believe me, take a look.

Before I could respond, I felt Gina in my head blocking Bobbi's images from coming through. I did not even know how to do that. Last time it happened was when Everett did it on Centauri to keep the locals from digging through my memories during our hearing before the High Council. Michelle obviously had been working overtime in mentoring her adopted little sister.

"We'll take your word for it, Bobbi." Gina replied. "Jimmy's one of those superstitious Irishmen. We'll both wait until the birth to see the baby."

"Suit yourself," Bobbi responded in kind. "Just tell your man to take a breath, before he gives himself a heart attack with all his baby worry."

She turned back to me, "and no, Jimmy, don't worry, you're not having a heart attack!" She took a long sip from her coffee cup, then deadpanned. "You're going to be hit by a milk truck."

Both Whitey and Lenny guffawed in unison.

"You had that coming." Everett added.

Maeve and Blue suddenly sprang to their feet and bolted around the side of the house.

"That would be Eileen." Bobbi said, grabbing her shawl from the back of her chair and following them.

"I better get back down to the barn," Claire said and then trotted off in that direction.

"You and Jimmy go ahead," Helen said. "The rest of us will clear this up."

Michelle appeared at our side with our coats. "I'm going with them," she said. "Everett, you stay here and help with the dishes."

Gina took my hand. *Smile, sweetie. You heard Bobbi; it's all going to be just fine.*

Before the three of us reached the side gate, carefully moving at human pace, Bobbi had returned down the hill with Dr. Eileen Cotto. The doc was shorter than I expected, although I had only viewed images of her sitting around the table at The Oracle. She was dressed in a green padded coverall and wore knee high, rubber muck boots. Her silver-blond hair was tucked beneath one of those Canadian looking ear-flap hats. She was carrying an old-fashioned leather Doctor's bag with Eileen Cotto, DVM stenciled in gold lettering on one side.

Bobbi made the introductions.

"Eileen, these are my dear friends Gina and Jimmy, Claire's –"

"– Servants!" I said, stepping forward and offering Eileen my hand. I could hear Claire's Lurchy laughter coming in response from the direction of the barn. I am not sure what it is with lesbians and handshakes, but Eileen's would have crushed my human hand.

"Perfect for dragging recalcitrant calves from exhausted cows," Bobbi chimed in.

As Gina stepped forward to greet her, Eileen performed the once over with a professional eye. Before I had the chance to feel jealous, Eileen took an extended look at Gina's belt-line through her open jacket and piped in "Congratulations. You look about twelve weeks along."

Gina blushed.

"Sorry," Eileen apologized. "Occupational hazard."

"I mentioned that Eileen was a midwife in Cali for ten years before packing it in and heading out to Vet School here in Colorado." Bobbi reminded us.

"I can call a pregnancy to within a week, either way. Never been wrong." Eileen boasted.

"And this is our good friend and neighbor Michelle," I said, trying to shift the conversation away from Gina's pregnancy. I hooked my thumb behind me. Eileen and Michele nodded across my shoulder in acknowledgment.

Have a feeling this may be one of her "first time for everything" days. Michele relayed to the rest of us telepathically.

Eileen looked around. "Now where is this mule Bobbi's been telling me about?"

I directed her through the side gate and pointed towards the barn. Bobbi led the way. Claire appeared in the doorway just as we arrived and gave Eileen her own version of the once over. *Turnabout is fair play.*

"Oh, she's a beautiful animal." Eileen cooed as she approached.

Got that right! Claire shared telepathically. Bobbi giggled.

"Do you have a halter for her?" Eileen asked.

I racked my brain. I had not seen Claire's halter since the day I brought her home from Mrs. Reynold's farm almost two years before.

It's hanging in the back corner of the stall. Claire messaged.

"Let me get it," Michelle said as she disappeared inside, returning moments later with halter in hand.

I took the dust covered halter from Michelle, slid it up over Claire's crinkling nose and hitched the top knot. Claire winked at me and I almost giggled.

"Just tie her off at the closest post," Eileen pointed while she fished through her bag on the ground with her other hand. Moments later she retrieved an old-school, industrial sized, glass bulb thermometer which she wiped with an alcohol swab before shaking it with the snap of her wrist. Before Claire knew what was happening, Eileen had closed the distance, lifted the base of her tail, and slid the cold thermometer home.

"Whoa," Claire bellowed, "you better buy me dinner after that move, sister."

Luckily, Michelle moved fast enough to catch the fainting Eileen before she hit the ground. Gina caught the falling thermometer before it disappeared into the snow.

CHAPTER SEVEN
(Come on Eileen - Ta Ooh La La)

Moving at Centauri speed, Michelle carried Eileen back up under the deck and placed her gently on the now empty table. Gina materialized beside them carrying the thermometer and Eileen's bag. She was rifling through its contents while I traveled between floors and returned from the Tower with the large red-cross bag Lenny had given us the night of the Storm. By the time Bobbi and Claire caught up with us, Gina had popped an ammonia nitrate ampule and waved it under Eileen's nose. As the veterinarian came to, she stared up at us all like Dorothy upon her return to Kansas.

"Didn't mean to frighten you back there," Claire apologized.

"Holy shit!" Eileen moaned, as she cleared the cobwebs from her brain. "You can talk." She scanned the group for Bobbi's face.

"I was hoping to ease you into that bit," Bobbi offered.

Eileen pulled herself up into a sitting position holding onto Gina's arm, and the rest of us backed away to give her some air. Eileen kept her eyes fixed on Claire the whole time.

"You could have given me a heads up, before sliding that icicle up my ass," Claire said defensively.

To everyone's surprise, Eileen started to laugh. Not a chuckle, but a full belly laugh, the kind of contagious laugh that spreads like a virus to everyone within the sound of it. And this one did just that. Even Claire joined in with her Lurchy sounding laugh.

After about thirty seconds Eileen caught her breath and said, "Bobbi, you crazy bitch, you almost gave me a heart attack."

"Well," Bobbi responded, "first off, that's Witch, with a 'W', not a 'B'. Second, now that we have gotten past that little hiccup, I need you to deliver an alien baby for me."

CHAPTER EIGHT
(All For One)

Lenahan poured a shot of Macallan and offered it to Eileen, "Here ya go, get this in ya, you've had a bit of a shock."

Eileen snatched it, threw it down the hatch and shuddered. "Oooh, that's good! Thanks." She whispered.

Despite the warmth from the heaters, Helen wrapped a large wool blanket around Eileen's shoulders and then gently guided her from the tabletop to one of the chairs.

Eileen's eyes then followed Bobbi's introductions of the remaining crew members who were assembled around the table, the way an infant's does when it first starts to recognize the voices of its family, not quite in focus, but showing a semblance of a connection.

She was obviously a lot tougher than her fainting spell suggested, because she seemed to assimilate the intimate details Bobbi was sharing without the expectant sensory overload, although she motioned to Lenny for a two-fingered refill when Bobbi mentioned Whitey's lycanthropy. When Bobbi introduced Michelle and Everett, they dematerialized on the far end of the table, appeared one either side of Eileen, patted her gently on each shoulder and then reappeared back at their original location. Eileen smiled in wonder.

Her mind kept reflecting images of Christmases from her childhood, acceptance of the magic without challenge.

"Well, that just leaves you two," Eileen said, gesturing in our direction.

"Yes," Bobbi responded, "you've met Jimmy and Gina, our resident alien hybrids."

Given the way things had spontaneously unfolded, without our ability to first feel her out and assess her discretion, I wanted to regain control of the situation, so I cut to the chase.

"Bobbi has vouched for you," I said, "but we've risked a lot letting you peek behind the curtain –"

"— Lighten up Macho Man." Eileen cut me off, regaining the control of her world. "No risk, no reward."

She stood up and slowly walked over to where Gina was standing and placed her hand on Gina's belly. Gina smiled.

"I was afraid that at my age there were no more surprises left in my life." Eileen turned and looked around at all of our expectant faces. "Let's just call this my last great adventure. I'm in."

"Well, that's a relief," Michelle chimed in, "I really didn't want to have to drop you in Crater lake."

CHAPTER NINE
(Prenatal On Steroids)

I was quick to learn that no one could ever accuse Eileen of being shy. Within two weeks, I had spent over thirty-grand on a dictated list of medical equipment that included a *SonoScape S2 Portable Ultrasound System,* and *Corometrics 172 Fetal Monitor,* an *Optimum-UV Enlight system*, and a *Hill-Rom Affinity III Birthing Bed,* along with an array of medical bits and bobs. She even had me order a *La Bassine* inflatable birthing pool just in case Gina decided to go in that direction. Enlisting Whitey's personal human skillset, Eileen quickly converted one of the first-floor guest bedrooms into a birthing room with warm colors and lighting. She even had him run a devoted electric line from the main fuse box to make sure that her power demands would not be interrupted.

During this set-up time, Eileen grilled Michelle on everything she knew about the Centauri gestation and birthing process, establishing the commonality with its human counterpart and calculating the anticipated adjustments. She came away from those sessions with surprising confidence. Some people are just naturals.

Personally, despite Bobbi's continuous representations that it was all going to be okay, I was scared shitless.

By the end of the second week of January, the belly and all other relevant parts of the now clearly pregnant looking Gina was covered in gel, resting in that birthing bed, as Eileen deftly maneuvered the hand-held transducer in search of its occupant while never taking her eyes off the monitor. I was becoming hypnotized by the recurring strong swooshing beat emanating from the ultrasound machine, which resembled a tricked-out laptop, with a few additional bells-and-whistles, and digital numbers across the top and bottom of the screen.

"That swishing sound you are hearing is the healthy heartbeat of your son." Eileen commented, as she circled the globe. "C'mon now, show yourself my prince."

There was a flutter of movement as she centered over her target.

"There you are young man." She adjusted the transducer. "Well, aren't you a big boy."

The fetus looked about 8 inches in length and had developed facial features, ears, fingers, and toes. His head was surprisingly erect, not the curved shrimp look I was expecting, and his limbs were moving.

I peeked into Eileen's mind and, after sifting through the incomprehensible medical terminology flowing through her analysis, pulled the only thing I wanted to know – *He looks healthy as an ox* – which I assumed that, coming from a vet, the "ox" analogy was a good thing.

I felt Michele rifling through my mind to recover the screen images and the "ox" prognosis, before receiving the Centauri's glowing assessment. *He's beautiful.*

Gina started to weep as she gazed upon this miracle. I was overwhelmingly numb, as I just could not process that this was really happening. And yet, there it was, right on the screen in front of me. I reached up to my face and felt that my beard was soaked with tears.

"Given that this is the first Centaurian baby I have ever midwifed, we are going to have to carefully monitor his growth on a daily basis so that I can get a better understanding of just how far along you are. As it is now, this fellow looks about 20 weeks in the human gestation model."

She gave Gina a careful visual assessment and then concluded. "Lucky for you that you have those wide, Italian, breeder's hips. You're going to need them."

CHAPTER TEN
(The Calm Before)

In my humble opinion, there must have been a woman behind the Big Bang, because every woman I have ever met demonstrates an innate ability to bring order out of chaos. Helen, Bobbi and now Eileen took over my home, and with the assistance of the extraterrestrial Michelle, quickly rendered me redundant. I had served my procreative function, and was now gently instructed to stand aside, stop worrying, and let the experts handle it from here. So, for the next two months, I did just that.

But what my six-plus decades of experience has also taught me, is that men inherently love chaos. We are lightning rods for it. Chaos seeks and finds us. My life until now had been a textbook example of this hypothesis. There must be some quantum theorem to explain it all. If not, when someone does discover it, I hope they name it after me.

Other than Claire, the females of all species pretty much politely ignored me. The core group of wife, lesbians and extraterrestrial would all gather on the first floor every day and run through their medical tests and processes each morning in the birthing room and then expand into the rest of the first floor for food, drink, and laughter. Lots of laughter. And the most annoying part was that every time I heard them laughing, I was blocked from dipping into their heads to see what was so funny. They even blocked me from entering Eileen's head. When the weather permitted, they all donned their winter coats and boots and walked the property with Claire.

Even my sister, Bonnie, and her spouse Tessa, had free access to Gina's daily telepathic updates from across the pond, given their lifetime lesbian membership and roles as the fairy godmothers. However, in female solidarity they refused to share anything beyond, "not to worry, baby and momma are fine. Sorry, must ring off, ta." Those lesbians truly know how to keep a secret.

So, I went about my business. I day traded when I needed a distraction. Thanks to my already nimble human intellect and my acquired ability to process information at Centauri digital speeds, and a little intuition that must have rubbed off on me from Bobbi, I made so much money I had to start getting more and more creative in hiding it overseas. I started establishing and fully funding offshore, irrevocable trusts, that would ensure that any of my descendants, direct or lateral, would be as wealthy as Croesus. I also funded another corporate trust that retained and paid the most creative Gibraltar law firms, to make sure that the money ultimately found its way into the right hands. I felt like the tiny Monopoly man, all I needed was the morning suit, top hat, and cane.

The rest of the time, I fixed things around the property. With Whitey's help, I renovated Geppetto's studio. First Whitey dug the trenches and ran an upgraded electric line to provide more power to run all the toys, warm board electric heating and an air conditioning system. Then we added a small bathroom, which we tied into the existing waste line running through the back property. We had soon turned it into an awesome man cave. We even included an oversized entranceway, just so Claire could enter if she desired. Of course, when I finally had my man cave grand opening, Everett pointed out over his third tumbler of Macallan, that none of the attendees, except Eddie and Lenny, would, technically speaking, qualify as human male, so mancave was a misnomer. So, I christened my renovated studio the more species inclusive and gender neutral "Two Mule Salon" in honor of Claire and Mister Rogers.

Everett tried to distract me during this period by organizing a weekly boys' night out where, Lenny, Whitey, Everett, Eddie and I would stop into the Side Tracked bar in Berthoud for some beers and bullshit. The owners, Jim and Maureen Barnett, were friendly but were respectful of our privacy and, after ensuring that we were situated at a large table in the furthest corner of the room, maintained a steady flow of all the food and drink we desired, then left us to our own devices until closing time. Whitey regularly volunteered to be the designated driver, as he worried that being drunk in public could lead to an unintended transformation. Lenny and Everett liked to annoy some of the regulars by taking their money in dart games. Lenny had a natural ability to find the center of the board. But if the games ever got too close, Everett just cheated by using his Centaurian speed to place the dart wherever he needed, without ever appearing to leave his spot, 7 feet, 9 and a quarter inches from the board. Realizing that I had corrupted this Centaurian beyond redemption by my human *win at all costs* mentality, I started forcing him to intentionally lose on occasion, just to keep the locals sated.

I tried to use this time at Side Tracked to rifle through Everett's mind, usually when he was focused on his dart game, but unfortunately found after a couple of attempts that Michelle had also relegated him to what I had taken to calling "mushroom status." We were both fungi that were kept in the dark and fed shit.

When we were alone, Claire would take pity on me and share a basic summary of the day's developments, physical and otherwise, but maintained her loyalty to the dominant gender by mentally blocking me from delving in her mind for any follow-up. One time, when I was out cleaning her barn, she suddenly burst into laughter in that Lurchy way of hers, and when I pressed her, she responded, "I can't, I can't, it's a girl thing, but that Eileen has some really funny stories."

Each night, I would sit with my ever-expanding spouse in the Tower and subtly employ my most effective lawyer interrogation skills to try and ferret out what she and her crew did all day long, but she would only telepathically provide me with the basic essentials.

I'm fine, the baby is fine, we're fine. Relax, we got this.

Like Claire, Gina would not betray the sisterhood and blocked me from delving any deeper on my own. She became very good at distracting me, whenever my agitation surfaced, by taking my hand and placing it on her belly. My son, hidden within, an obvious sympathizer of the feminine cabal, would kick and run his hands across her skin on cue, allowing me to count fingers and tickle feet, just enough to feel invested in the process, but when I tried to delve into his ever-developing mind, I found it blocked by the ferociously protective Gina. Then Gina would lay down on the bed and revert to the very human process of sleeping, *for the good of the baby*, leaving me wide awake to ponder the imponderable. Once mother and child had entered the realm of Hypnos, the god of sleep, their minds were safely beyond my telepathic reach.

This provided an instant recipe for male frustration and paranoia.

By the end of March, I was at my breaking point. But right on cue, Chaos came knocking.

CHAPTER ELEVEN
(EVERETT'S HOBBY)

Since the 1940s, Everett's mission on behalf of his Centauri people, and evidently the rest of the citizens of the universe, was to generally keep an eye on the humans. This was particularly true when it came to their unending wars, just to ensure that they did not destroy the planet. His main job though was to make sure they did not get ahead of themselves once they started exploring space. In fact, it was Everett's mancave collection of pillaged parts from some of the spacecrafts and satellites he had disabled over the years that first tipped me off that there was something very different about my closest neighbor on Beverly Drive.

After our return to earth following Everett's successful appeal before the Centauri High Council, which almost landed me back with my dead brothers on the other side of the veil, Everett was, for all intents and purposes, given early retirement with a great pension package, including keeping Jayney, his spacecraft, and Michele's smaller version of the same. Given that our world was still a really dangerous place, I just assumed that the Centauries had installed a replacement zoo keeper. If they did, Everett never mentioned it.

The retired Everett could only do so much fishing, which he really sucked at, so he went back to doing what he did best, but on a purely personal hobby basis. That meant he constantly scanned the internet, regular and dark web, followed every news feed he could access, and literally dipped into the minds of every major politician of every major country, and some minor ones, with the dexterity of the Artful Dodger. He even took Jayney on a few road trips to get a bird's eye view of some of the things he read about first-hand. As a result, no one of any consequence on this planet farted without Everett getting a first whiff.

Personally, I could not give a rat's ass about what was happening out in the world around me, as long as I had what I needed, and the world left Jimmy Moran and his loved ones alone. After we relegated the shrunken remnants of the Valachi family to the bottom of Crater Lake two years before, I drew my circle even tighter, and stopped even asking Lenny, who still collected his government paycheck as a U.S. Marshall working with WITSEC, for updates from his government contacts on the east coast. As long as my family of misfits were happy, the world could go to hell.

And it turns out, it was doing just that.

I only half listened whenever Everett shared any topical news with me, either aurally, if in person, and telepathically in English. However, if there was a lot of information to be shared quickly, Everett would download it to me through telepathic digital transmission. While I enjoyed mastering the practical digital language that was the common method of communication among the Centaurians, I found it emotionally sterile, without the beauty of nuance that even a telepathically shared English word could provide. Even after all of my preternatural humans and Claire were able to pick up digital communication through what Bobbi had dubbed cross-pollinating when we engaged telepathically as a group after my return from space, the novelty soon wore off. I reverted to communicating in person aurally, unless expediency or distance required an alternate approach. Still, I remained open to and engaged in whatever form of communication any of the misfit family chose to employ. All knowledge is useful, and information is power.

Everett began to share stories that he was following about a pair of genius twins, Victor and Seth Beauseigneur, who had left MIT after three years and developed this Artificial Intelligence platform they called Cas-Lux, that was purportedly about to take the world by storm. The tech industry media was buzzing with predictions of all kinds of applications in basically every industry, including the military industrial complex, which instantly lifted their start-up company, Gemini-2.N - G2N on NASDAQ - to the heady realm of the alphabet tech oligarchies. I retained just enough of this information to execute a substantial purchase of that company's IPO through a number of my overseas accounts. That investment quadrupled in value overnight and had continued to rise since then. The twins were instant billionaires. I did not do too badly either.

As a result, I paid a little more attention to Everett's stories about these particular twins, not because I cared one iota about them as humans, that number was limited to those humans presently circulating among my misfit family, but because I like to protect my investments.

According to Everett, these twins were a closed circuit. Orphaned at eighteen when their parents died in a gas explosion while they were at school, they were not married, did not date, and only socialized with each other. They had been recently quoted in one of the leading tech journals as saying that communicating with anyone else was so distasteful, their brain cells started to self-destruct. Thus, their only interaction with outsiders was limited to purely business. Their only passionate legacy was the AI program that they had developed, which purportedly made the ubiquitous AI home interfaces of their alphabet company predecessors, with feminine names and sultry voices, look like mechanical wind-up toys from the 1930s. And the reach of their AI was as endless as the Internet itself, it could purportedly subjugate most other programs at will. Indeed, the Grimm Twins, as I liked to call them, recently installed their AI program as their go-to buffer between them and everyone else. The world communicated with their AI, and the AI communicated with the twins. Everett said that one on-line blogger had claimed that the twins had actually surgically installed DNA based biological circuit chips in their brains that allowed them to telepathically communicate with each other and their AI program. Nothing happened in this world without the Grimm Twins learning of it.

These brothers used some of their newly acquired wealth to purchase a five-thousand-acre ranch outside of Baker Oregon, with a modern compound that included an eight thousand square foot mansion, with views of the Eagle Cap Mountains, a thirty-unit bunkhouse, horse barn, workshop and hay shed, all behind a locked gate at end of a mile long private lane off a county road. There was a hundred-acre proglacial lake in the center of the property, whose perimeter was bordered by the Wallowa-Whitman National Forest. The twins immediately installed upgrades that included a helipad to land their *Vantablack* Sikorsky S-92, and a landing strip long enough to accommodate their Gulfstream III.

The combination of that level of genius, wealth and reclusiveness fed the internet rumor mill and the unsupported speculation that the brothers were the next rung of humanoid on the evolutionary ladder, and were into everything from the occult to adrenochrome. Rumor also had it that the brothers liked to toy with the lesser humans by funding a number of subversive anarchist groups that wreaked havoc out in the real world, which kept the media and government from paying any concerted attention to what they were doing behind closed doors.

These two are trouble, was the last communication Everett shared on the subject.

The sudden loss of the Binary Beauseigneur updates was not because Everett had lost interest in the two telepathically conjoined geniuses, but because Everett's focus was now laser sharp on news of the viral pandemic that had purportedly originated in a lab in Wuhan, China and was now rapidly spreading across the world.

CHAPTER TWELVE
(Apocalypse Now)

The world began to shut down during the last month of Gina's pregnancy. Everett explained that this viral variant, dubbed COVID-19, was reportedly highly contagious and had a quick and serious impact on those humans that were of advanced age or suffered some other pre-morbidity marker such as a heart condition, asthma, or diabetes. Generally, it did not seem to impact young healthy children, who, if infected, appeared asymptomatic, and the average overall survival rate for all other age groups was north of 99 percent. Everett assured me that Centaurians and us hybrids were immune to all human viruses, whatever their source. So, it posed no threats to Gina or the baby. I stopped worrying about it before I ever started.

But given this was an election year in the United States, I knew that this pandemic was going to be the political football for the remainder of the year.

My years as a mafia lawyer taught me to not get too caught up with who was purportedly running the country. Elections only made a difference to those people who were forced to play by the government's rules. I did not do so as a member of the Valachi family, and I was not now. I had created a new life after WITSEC that allowed for a public façade of Jimmy Moran, who earned a few hundred thousand a year as a day trader using his traceable trading accounts, which was happily shared with whatever political party chose to take their slice. But my civic good will existed only because I had access to what was now, thanks to my mafia earnings and Centaurian abilities, close to half a billion dollars in untraceable offshore money. But to be perfectly honest, I have always had a problem with other assholes spending my money for me, no matter what political party they came from. Charity begins at home.

The resulting stay at home orders immediately imposed by most states, including Colorado, caused our band of misfits very limited inconvenience. For the most part, we had always isolated at home, did not attend church, had no children of school age, and could continue to purchase what we needed at the major, big box, stores that had received some strange governmental dispensation that allowed them to continue operating, while the mom-and-pop stores were forced to close, some forever. Whitey's construction company was classified as an "essential" business, and he was actually busier than ever as people used money they had set-aside for travelling and dining out to make improvements they might otherwise have left to a future time, if they were not spending all of their time working and staying at home. Whitey ensured, through his construction-based talents, that their "staycations" were bearable.

I used a series of cut-out, international corporations to Smurf numerous small amounts of money into offshore trust accounts for Helen, Bobbi, and Eddie, and provided them with instructions on how to draw from them as needed. I also provided them with contact numbers for the appropriate members of the Gibraltar law firms that were managing those trusts. I made sure that there was enough in Helen's trust to cover the losses from her shuttered restaurant and to keep paying the three Sirens during the shutdown.

Given that their respective blood families were not taking any chances with the pandemic, Gina was forced to maintain her daily contact with the younger, human members of our group through facetime and texts. If she did not have the distraction of the upcoming birth, the sudden loss of physical access to Scarlett, Savanna and Lucian might have broken her heart.

Eileen limited her veterinarian practice to late afternoon office hours and the occasional emergent situation with existing clients that required Eileen to go out on a call. The rest of her time she spent with the women, with an occasional common meal appearance by the five members of the group with outdoor plumbing. She got along with everyone, but still would not divulge what was going on behind the birthing room door.

In short, I felt a little like Rick Blaine, the fictional ex-patriot played in the film version by Humphrey Bogart who continued to run his nightclub in

Casablanca, Morocco as he saw fit while the rest of the world was going to hell during the early stages of WWII.

What happened outside my home in Berthoud did not concern me and I did not give a damn about who was running the rest of the world.

But then Chaos walked right through my front door. And it did not give a shit about the rest of this world either.

CHAPTER THIRTEEN
(An Uninvited Guest)

My mother used to tell me that nothing good ever happens to you after midnight. Of course, that was when I was a teenager and was fighting with my parents on a daily basis to extend my curfew past that magic hour. Looking back, she was wrong, because since that time, some absolutely amazing things happened to me in the wee hours of a new day. But, as they say, even a broken clock is right twice every twenty-four hours.

By the third week of March, Gina's abdomen had expanded to dimensions that would only be comfortably supported walking with a small, gardener's wheelbarrow in front of her. She was relegated by her ladies in waiting to complete bed rest and slept in the first-floor master suite directly adjoining the birthing room. With nothing better to do, including sleep, Michelle kept night watch in the recliner in the corner of that bedroom. Eileen had commandeered the Tower's master bedroom suite, and Helen and Bobbi began sleeping on the pull-out bed on the king-sized convertible sofa on the basement level. I was the ghost in the building, invisible to everyone else, and spent most nights roaming the hallways, the property and visiting with Claire. But as Claire still needed her forty winks, my visits were kept brief and to the point. I felt as useless as the pulled pin of a grenade, my job was done, I just had to sit back and wait for the explosion.

Spring had officially arrived in Colorado on March 19, 2020, and the consistent white landscape of fallen snow began to cede the earth back its greenery. By the early morning of March 23rd, all the snow, like Elvis, had left the area.

I spent the nocturnal hours of that new day wandering the property in the darkness of the new moon and driving Claire crazy by repeatedly interrupting her sleep cycle. On my third visit to her lair in the space of an hour she finally called me on it.

"Jimmy, you gotta let a girl get her beauty sleep," Claire mumbled crankily from the blackness of the furthest reaches of the stall area. "When you're my age, looking this good every day takes effort, and lots of sleep."

"Well, maybe I wouldn't be such a pain in the ass, if this Ass would be more forthcoming as to what exactly is happening with my wife and child-to-be." I responded, just a bit testily.

"I've told you the last two times you woke me, Gina's –"

"– fine, the baby's fine, we're fine." I completed the mantra.

"Anything beyond that is above my pay grade." Claire stated resolutely, her loyalty to the mystical sisterhood, at least at this moment, unwavering.

I was about to push back when I received a transmission from Everett.

01001010 01101001 01101101 01101101 01111001 00101100
00100000 01100111 01100101 01110100 00100000 01101111
01110110 01100101 01110010 00100000 01101000 01100101
01110010 01100101 00101100 00100000 01110111 01100101
00100000 01101000 01100001 01110110 01100101 00100000
01100011 01101111 01101101 01110000 01100001 01101110
01111001 00101110 00001010

Jimmy, get over here, we have company.

I materialized in front of their property and spotted a faint blue glow silhouetting the house. I had not seen that lighting since the morning I stowed away on Everett's spacecraft, Jayney, during our last trip to Centauri. Without conscious effort, I materialized beside Everett in the open area directly behind his mancave building. He was taking the final hit on a fragrant roach for Dutch courage, as he stared, unblinking, at the Class A RV-sized spaceship that was resting before him. Its plasma shield was still in place.

"That's not Jayney." I whispered, rhetorically.

The glow from the plasma and the craft itself suddenly disappeared, leaving only the massive shadow in the center of an already dark landscape. I felt it more than saw it, and it felt like a black hole. The energy emanating from within the vehicle was palpable.

"Perfect," came a disembodied voice that invoked my misophonic response, like fingernails across chalkboards, "You're both here."

CHAPTER FOURTEEN
(Interstellar)

Aldor materialized out of the darkness in all of his glory, his perfect Centaurian features wrapped in floor-length robes flowing in the slightest of breezes coming off the foothills. He gazed around with the judgmental look of a mother-in-law coming to visit your home for the first time and being less than impressed. *Been there, done that.*

"Vocal communication. Nice entrance." I barked.

When in Rome. He responded telepathically. I immediately blocked his ability to pilfer my thoughts. *Once bitten.*

Some emotions are just visceral. Standing before me was a perfect being who did everything in his power during our last encounter on Centauri to ensure that my 're-animation' as he called it, was reversed and that I would never return to earth. The death sentence on his planet. I hated this guy with all my being and had to consciously suppress my rising urge to smash his nose, as I had done during Everett's hearing before the Centauri High Council. Even without access to my mind, he must have felt my angry energy because his hand rose protectively to his face.

Citizen Aldor, to what do I owe the pleasure of your visit? Everett transmitted with the diffusive calm of a sated pothead.

I'm not here to 'visit.' Aldor responded telepathically.

"Well then," I said aurally, "Don't let our atmospheric door hit you on the ass on your way out."

As proof of my theory that the sound of the spoken word carries nuances that can be lost in other forms of transmission, Aldor recoiled at the sting of my comment. Everett chuckled like a stoner.

You really have gone native, Everett. Aldor transmitted, his eyes delivering his contempt.

"Thank you." Everett responded, punctuating his statement with another chuckle.

Enough of this! Aldor transmitted, his imperiousness subtle, but present.

He stared at me with the suppressed joy of someone who is about to regain the upper hand.

Petrichor sends her fond regards to you, her Jimmy Moran. Aldor transmitted his obviously rehearsed line without taking his eyes off me. *She sends you her love, by which I mean she sends you your daughter. . . Interstellar.*

At that moment, a tiny glow sparked directly beside Aldor and instantly ignited into a full flash of brilliant golden light. When my eyes adjusted, there standing beside Aldor, was an angelic young girl, that looked about three years of human age, with translucent, alabaster skin and burgundy colored hair that flowed like filaments down and around her shoulders. Her blue eyes actually sparkled with their golden flecks around the pitch of her pupils.

Hello, father. In English, no numbers. Petrichor had taught her well. But my theory was wrong. I could feel the sweetness in her voice just through her telepathic transmission. *Mother sends her love.*

Aldor was savoring my physical response to his magic act.

01010000 01100101 01110100 01110010 01101001 01100011
01101000 01101111 01110010 00100000 01110111 01100001
01101110 01110100 01110011 00100000 01111001 01101111
01110101 00100000 01110100 01101111 00100000 01110010
01100001 01101001 01110011 01100101 00100000 01001001
01101110 01110100 01100101 01110010 01110011 01110100
01100101 01101100 01101100 01100001 01110010 00100000
01100001 01110011 00100000 01100001 00100000 01101000
01110101 01101101 01100001 01101110 00100000 01100011
01101000 01101001 01101100 01100100 00101100 00100000
01110111 01101001 01110100 01101000 00100000 01100001
01101100 01101100 00100000 01101111 01100110 00100000

01111001 01101111 01110101 01110010 00100000 01101101
01101001 01110011 01100111 01110101 01101001 01100100
01100101 01100100 00100000 01110000 01100001 01110011
01110011 01101001 01101111 01101110 00100000 01100001
01101110 01100100 00100000 01111010 01100101 01100001
01101100 00100000 01100110 01101111 01110010 00100000
01101100 01101001 01100110 01100101 00101110 00100000
00100000 01010011 01101000 01100101 00100000 01110111
01101001 01101100 01101100 00100000 01100010 01100101
00100000 01110111 01100001 01110100 01100011 01101000
01101001 01101110 01100111 00101110 00100000 00100000

Petrichor wants you to raise Interstellar as a human child, with all of your misguided passion and zeal for life. She will be watching.

With that, Aldor turned and bowed respectfully towards the little girl, then dematerialized. A moment later the spacecraft came to life, and the plasma shield reengaged. I reflexively snatched the child protectively in my arms and materialized a safe distance away from the animated craft. As we watched it maximize its power, I received the finely nuanced, parting telepathic transmission from the scumbag Aldor:

01000010 01100101 01110111 01100001 01110010 01100101
00100000 01110100 01101000 01100101 00100000 01101100
01100001 01110111 00100000 01101111 01100110 00100000
01110101 01101110 01101001 01101110 01110100 01100101
01101110 01100100 01100101 01100100 00100000 01100011
01101111 01101110 01110011 01100101 01110001 01110101
01100101 01101110 01100011 01100101 01110011 00101100
00100000 01001010 01101001 01101101 01101101 01111001
00100000 01001101 01101111 01110010 01100001 01101110
00100001 00100000 00100000 00001010

Beware the law of unintended consequences, Jimmy Moran!

CHAPTER FIFTEEN
(No Language Can Withstand a Real Bronx Accent)

The child and I watched as the still very stoned Everett followed Aldor's silent lift off and meteoric ascent into the moonless night, his thoughts free to those who could receive them.

Never actually got the chance to observe a take-off like that, very cool!

He continued to stare into the night. *That Aldor's a real asshole.*

He chuckled at his own thoughts.

After another moment, Everett remembered he was not alone, looked over and then materialized beside us. He held out his open palm, and the girl reached out and placed her palm within his.

"Interstellar," he said softly, "what a pretty name."

Mommy gave me that name because I connect two stars. She responded telepathically with an unexpected maturity. *Mommy's and Daddy's.* With that she turned back to me, wrapped her arms tightly around my neck and buried her face into my chest. I was suddenly overwhelmed by a digital download of thousands of waves of her memories, from her first suckling on Petrichor's breast immediately after birth to the last moment with her mother on Centauri, releasing her final embrace and taking the hand of Aldor outside the spaceship. I could not focus on them individually as they appeared as a lightning stream of numeric zeros and ones in one massive download and did not seem to pass directly into my mind but instead, entered through my heart. I audibly gasped from the experience.

I felt like my chest was going to burst and physically cried out her name to make her stop, but butchered by my Bronx accent it came out, "Inta. . . . Stella!"

"Stella!" Everett mimicked the last word out loud, capturing its Bronx nuance like he had grown up on Arthur Avenue, his stoned mind fixated on the minutia of the moment. "It means 'star' in Greek," he leaned over and kissed her hand. "Yes, that will work just fine. A much more human sounding name."

"Stel-la," the tiny girl repeated slowly and cautiously, surprised at the sound of her own voice. It was clearly recognizable in its match in tone and beauty to her mother's.

"I know we weren't attached to the hip up on Centauri," Everett said with a Cheshire grin, "but is there anything you forgot to mention?"

"See for yourself." I opened my mind and felt him rifling through my memories of our trip to Centauri, right through and including my blacking out immediately after Petrichor propositioned me. Then I allowed him to review my memories of the floating infant during our return through the wormhole and finally the cryptic message from Petrichor just before I awoke Christmas morning.

"As far as I can tell, you might have gotten close, but there was no cigar."

Everett studied the girl's facial features carefully. Then he scrutinized my face with the same intensity, to the point that I was starting to feel uncomfortable. He reached up and ran his fingers through my beard and along my jawline, resting their tips on the end of my chin. His eyes lit up in recognition.

"She has your chin!"

Given that I have never been considered 'a looker,' I drew some solace from the fact that if she had to be saddled with any of my features, my strong chin would never fail her as her last defense to a fast fist and would not otherwise detract too much from the remaining facial beauty she had inherited from her mother.

And she didn't get that hair from her Centauri side. Everett added.

My Ginger brother is probably laughing in heaven. And if she's got those same genes, she's going to need that chin.

"Does Gina know about this?" He asked out loud, fearing the worst.

I shook my head. "Until tonight, there wasn't anything to tell."

"Who is Gina?" Stella asked.

I pulled up visual memories of all of my happiest moments with my wife and telepathically shared them with the child. She smiled and my heart melted.

Is she going to be my earth mommy?

I felt Everett stepping into my mind and blocking any further access by Stella.

"Sorry, Jimmy, but this is above my pay grade," he said. "I'm calling in reinforcements."

A moment later, Michele appeared, numbers flying, looking a bit agitated for being called away from her night-watch post.

01010111 01101000 01100001 01110100 00100111 01110011
00100000 01110011 01101111 00100000 01101001 01101101
01110000 01101111 01110010 01110100 01100001 01101110
01110100 00100000 01110100 01101000 01100001 01110100
00100000 01111001 01101111 01110101 00100000 01101110
01100101 01100101 01100100 01100101 01100100 00100000
01101101 01100101 00100000 01101111 01110110 01100101
01110010 00100000 01101000 01100101 01110010 01100101
00100000 01110010 01101001 01100111 01101000 01110100
00100000 01100001 01110100 00100000 01110100 01101000
01101001 01110011 00100000 01101101 01101111 01101101
01100101 01101110 01110100 00111111 00001010 00001010

What's so important that you needed me over here right at this moment?

While she was dressed in a quintessentially human blue jean ensemble, there was no doubting Michele was a powerful, female Centaurian.

Stella's face reflected an instantaneous recognition of Michelle's close physical proximity to her mother and disappeared from my arms, reappearing in that same moment with her tiny body wrapped tightly around Michele's torso and neck.

"What the —"

Before Michele could finish her expletive, Everett had digitally downloaded Stella's entire backstory that led to this moment, including that Gina was totally unaware.

"Holy —," Michele fumbled for the right words as she grasped the young girl under her arms and held her out before her, like a new dress, giving the child the once over, "Moley! . . . Aren't you a cutey?"

Stella smiled and pulled herself back into a full embrace of Michele, then disappeared and reappeared in my arms.

What am I going to do? I asked Michele.

Michele reached over and lifted Stella back into her own embrace.

Better get your ass over there before Gina wakes up, then tell her everything. And I mean everything. Because this is one of those moments you're only going to get one shot at. So, don't blow it.

"Stella," Michele then said out loud, with an unexpectedly comforting tone to her voice, "would you like to come inside our house with Aunty Michele and Uncle Everett? Your daddy has to do something, but he'll be right back, I promise."

"You hope!" Everett added.

Stella looked over at me, then back at Michele and nodded.

The first red rays of the sun were reaching into the night sky and faint blue glow was rising from the eastern horizon.

And remember to block your mind so Gina doesn't ferret it out on her own before you tell her.

"Uncle Everett?" Michele said out loud, "Let's take Stella inside. Maybe you can show her some of your space junk."

"Good luck!" Everett called to me, before the three of them disappeared and a light went on inside their kitchen.

I took a fortifying breath and slowly started walking at human speed back towards my home.

Put the toilet seat down.

CHAPTER SIXTEEN
(*Mea Culpa*)

I remember as a kid that whenever I was compelled to own up to a big mistake to those in authority, and facing inevitable sanctions, first by my parents, then by the priests and nuns of St. Margaret's, I always said a silent prayer that some cataclysmic event would intercede and spare me of my burden. *Deus ex Machina*. My big three on my wish-list were always a biblical flood, an apocalyptic meteor strike, or an alien invasion. I never got the easy out.

As I slowly walked the quarter mile back towards my house, and towards my sleeping, extremely pregnant with our first child, Tellurian-Centaurian hybrid wife, I kept listening for the sound of rushing water and looking skyward for that ball of flame. I knew that the alien invasion was not going to save me, indeed, it had gotten me in this fix. *So, be careful what you wish for.*

I replayed the 'life with Gina' memories I had just offered Stella and then followed them with memories of all the bad shit I had dragged Gina through over the past half century. The mafia, the murder, my death, her involuntary transmutation. She asked for none of it, and accepted it all, because she loved me enough to do so.

Now, finally, through another miracle, as some form of consolation prize for her sacrifices, Gina was about to experience the one thing we could never do as humans. She was about to give birth to our child. One final first that was all ours. And I was about to change that dynamic.

When I got to the top of the driveway, I bit the bullet and materialized in the night watch chair abandoned by Michele in the corner of the first-floor master bedroom. Gina lay on her side, her large belly pushing against the large form of Blue, who was relegated to what would be my spot on the far side of the bed. Both wife and dog were snoring in syncopation, two shorter snores by Blue to each long snore by Gina.

I could not see into Gina's dreaming mind, and while I felt the energy emanating from our child in her belly, someone had blocked my ability to reach into his mind. Blue felt my presence, and soon her double note snores were replaced by the rapid beat of her tail beneath the covers. Was that the drum beat of celebration or war?

I felt Gina's stirring telepathic probe as she came to consciousness, but the toilet seat was down.

Her eyes opened slowly, and she peeked in my direction.

"Where's Michelle?" She asked, before grimacing from our son's sudden stirring in response to the sound of her voice. Blue was now totally awake, had freed herself from the blankets and was doing a perfect downward dog stretch on the floor beside the bed.

"She had an errand to run." I responded.

"And why have you closed your mind to me?"

I just could not find the words to start, and I realized that there was no way to spin this to my advantage, so I took the easy way out and digitally downloaded the entire story, right up to the memory of Michelle telling me not to do just that.

Gina's eyes bugged, her brows raised and knitted, and her mouth opened in horror as if she were witnessing a catastrophe in real time. I scanned her mind and saw her replaying it all at full digital speed, slowing only at the moments when Petrichor propositioned me and when Stella first addressed me as "father." When Gina realized I was eavesdropping she blocked me, shouting "get out!"

Before I could get to my feet, Gina screeched and suddenly the lower section of blankets became soaked on her side of the bed. If that was the biblical flood, it was too little, too late.

CHAPTER SEVENTEEN
(Sibling Symbiosis)

By the time I even thought about moving, Michelle had reappeared and handed me Stella, while Everett transported the three of us out of the room and into my living room. As dizzying as all of this was, Stella seemed unperturbed.

Was that my earth mommy? She asked me, with almost a clinical feel to her voice, while replaying her momentary view of Gina writhing on the bed.

I nodded. Helen and Bobbi flew up the stairs from the basement level just as Eileen arrived from the Tower. They all raced down the hallway like firefighters deploying at a firehouse.

I could hear Eileen barking out orders from the bedroom with military precision. "Michelle, get her into the birthing room and onto the bed. Helen, get that fetal monitor hooked up. Bobbi let's get those towels ready. C'mon ladies, just like I showed you, we have a baby to deliver."

And I could hear Gina's cries. I remembered one of Ty Valachi's associates, Enzo Ferangi, who recounted his experience witnessing the birth of his twin daughters, Chrissy and Cathy Tardibuono, to a group of us at a barbeque, that the pain a woman suffers when giving birth would be comparable to a man trying to shit out a pineapple.

Speaking from my own experience, if given a choice, I would rather be shot in the heart.

I also could hear the sounds of beeps and monitors. They became background noises, as Gina's voice remained my focus.

I was torn between my desire to be in the room with Gina, and my fear that my being there would only inflict more pain on her.

And every other woman's mind was on lockdown. Except, Claire, who reached out to me from the back yard.

I know you're frightened, Jimmy. But hang in there, the girls got this covered.

I immediately wanted to transport down and bury my face in Claire's neck for comfort.

Stay close to Gina and that beautiful girl of yours and wait it out. I'm looking forward to formal introductions when this is all behind us.

* * * * *

Hours passed and the sounds of Gina's cries from down the hallway grew louder and, at the same time, weaker. Everett offered to take Stella back to his place.

I'm staying here. She transmitted. I could sense her defiance.

Everett prepared some food and drinks for the three of us. Stella really took to the hot cocoa with mini marshmallows and ignored the sandwiches Everett prepared. Instead, she sampled from the bowl of mixed fruit he placed on the snack tray table before her. I too ignored the food but sipped the coffee just to distract myself.

Suddenly those background beeps and buzzes began to escalate, and I heard Eileen shout out something about "Variable Deceleration." Whatever that was, it did not sound good.

Michelle appeared beside me. For the first time since I met her, she looked afraid.

01010100 01101000 01100101 00100000 01100010 01100001
01100010 01111001 00100000 01101001 01110011 00100000
01101001 01101110 00100000 01110100 01110010 01101111
01110101 01100010 01101100 01100101 00101110 00100000
00100000 01000101 01101001 01101100 01100101 01100101
01101110 00100000 01101101 01100001 01111001 00100000
01101000 01100001 01110110 01100101 00100000 01110100
01101111 00100000 01110000 01100101 01110010 01100110
01101111 01110010 01101101 00100000 01100001 00100000
01000011 00101101 01010011 01100101 01100011 01110100
01101001 01101111 01101110 00101110

The baby is in trouble. Eileen may have to perform a C-Section.

At that moment, Stella disappeared.

I heard Eileen shout "get this kid out of the room!" Then everything went quiet.

As I materialized in the birthing room, I found everyone frozen in mid-movement and word, and as I fully appeared I became frozen as well. I could not speak, but I remained fully conscious and was able to see and hear. The same thing happened when Michelle and Everett appeared an instant later. Both Centaurians were in suspended animation. I could hear everyone's thoughts, which were flying haphazardly around the room as everyone was trying to figure out what was happening. All eyes were on Stella, who was up on the birthing bed besides the frozen Gina, running her tiny hands, which were now glowing with a pure white light, over Gina's exposed, distended stomach area. Stella's thoughts rose above the cacophony of all of the others with a calming dominance.

Come to me my baby brother.

Then, in the center of Gina's belly, a responsive, small oblong circle of the same bright white light began to form and as the light began to rise up against and then above Gina's skin, it took on the shape of an infant. When the light shape freed itself from its bond with its host, Stella gently grabbed hold of it and pulled it close to her, rolling backwards and landing on the blanket stretched like a hammock between Gina's legs, which were locked in the stirrups at the bottom of the bed.

The cry of a healthy baby's lungs simultaneously released everyone else in the room back into action, and after a moment of general acclimation, Stella released the baby into the reaching hands of Gina. Eileen rushed over to examine mother and child, while I swooped in to lift Stella off the birthing bed. But when I went to hand Stella to Michelle, she dematerialized and reappeared at the head of the bed next to Gina and the baby. When Gina realized the young girl was beside her, she reached her free arm out and pulled Stella into a scrum with her sibling.

Gina looked exhausted.

I reached out to her telepathically, *Are we okay? I swear I never . . .*

She nodded. *I just spent the last six hours replaying your memories repeatedly because I did not have a knife to bite on to distract me from my labor pain.*

She shared my brief memory of Dr. Nim, examining that tiny glass ampule of milky white liquid and then slipping it in her pocket. Then she replayed the memory when I finally turned down Petrichor's proposition.

You're off the hook. And besides, I might not be here at all if it wasn't for this little sweetheart stepping up to save her brother.

Gina gave Stella a soft kiss on her forehead, and Stella wrapped her arms around Gina's neck.

Saves me the trouble of going through that again to get my little girl.

"Lucky girl," Eileen chimed in, "no episiotomy or c-section! No scars! That's a win-win in my book."

"What should we call him?" Gina asked Stella.

"He told me his name is Apollo." Stella responded.

"Can't go wrong with a Greek god," Helen chimed in.

"Works for me." I responded.

"Then, Apollo it is!" Gina declared. Everyone cheered.

Eileen gently lifted the boy from Gina's lap and placed him in my arms. He had a full head of Burgundy hair, just like Stella. Fuck that Ginger gene. Luckily, like Stella, Apollo looked just like his mother, only his eyes were born Nordic blue.

"Okay daddy," Eileen said, retrieving the baby from my arms, "Times up. Mommy and baby need to rest."

I leaned over Gina and gave her a kiss.

Love ya. Love ya too.

I looked across at Stella and she materialized in my arms. This time I pulled her in tightly for a hug and she buried her face into my beard.

The others' thoughts were flying around the room.

Told you it was all going to work out! Bobbi exclaimed, throwing both hands in the air in a Victorious manner. *Do I know how to call it, or what! Shit, I better call Eddie and tell him to bring over lunch.*

That little lady is going to have to show her Aunty Michele how she performed that last little trick.

Congratulations one and all. When does Aunty Claire get to meet the children?

Off in the distance we could hear the howl of a lone wolf.

Whitey sends his love. Bobbi shared. *He'll be by after work.*

Then Lenny appeared in the door of the birthing room with a bottle of Macallan 18 and a fist full of Cohibas. "Helen called me this morning to give me the heads up, but I was down in Denver on some government business. Got here as soon as I could. What did I miss?"

CHAPTER EIGHTEEN
(It Takes A Family)

I never fully appreciated the concept of "family" until mine was taken away from me when Ty Valachi and his crew murdered my three brothers. Self-reliance is an important and laudable trait, but it is exhausting, lonely, and sometimes frightening. True family knows how to manage the balance between allowing its members to seek their own paths and chase their own dreams while always being in the ready to provide whatever backup and support is necessary. If a member of the family falls, the other members circle around and protect them until they are back on their feet. The success of one family member lifts the group – a rising tide floats all boats. If you fuck with a family member, the other members fuck you back. And you do not have to share bloodlines to be family.

Animals get this. They blend naturally to form herds, schools, flocks, and prides, all of them families, to ensure the continuation and success of their species. And that is a good thing. Because family is the only legacy that truly matters.

My Berthoud gathering of magical misfits was a text-book example of the concept of a blended family, consisting of an imperfect, yet seamless mix of blood and adopted members. Each one, including Eileen, had shown up just at the right moment, and had been drawn into a "quantum entanglement" with the others. Right out of the gate, they all circled around their newest members looking to imprint their knowledge and talents so that they too could be carried forth into the future. For each of these members, babies were a new thing, so they lined up to handle feedings, baby-sitting and, for the briefest of times, changing diapers. And I am not going to lie, I was happy to let them do it. Diaper changing is way overrated, especially after a few unexpected blasts with the urine hose.

The first thing I had to come to terms with, in my newest role as a biological parent in this family, was that genetic Centaurian children, and evidently their hybrids, develop differently than humans. As Michelle explained it, Centaurians are developmentally front-loaded, a bit like the animals on earth. They are physically, mentally, and emotionally matured in half the time as their purely human counterparts. So, by the approximate age of ten human years, a Centaurian has fully developed into adult status, when their aging process slowed to glacier speed. Hence, the five-hundred-year lifespan.

I found that concept a bit daunting since I was once one of those humans who suffered from a form of Peter Pan complex. Part of me never wanted to grow up. So, despite being physically and mentally in my sixties, I often displayed the emotional maturity of a ten-year-old. Fortunately, my resurrection as a Tellurian-Centaurian hybrid hit the biological reset button which allowed my stunted emotional development a chance to play catch-up. Emotional maturity still lagged behind, but at least it kept physical and mental maturity within striking distance.

I appreciated Michelle's Centaurian biology lesson because it prevented me from thinking I was losing it when every time I looked at Stella and Apollo, they appeared to change. At first, just a little, and later, a lot. Stella was a curious child, and I had to be careful to keep the mental toilet seat down, or I would find her rifling through my memory banks. And there were just some things I was not willing to share with her. Not yet. But I did share my memories of my interactions with her mother on Centauri, my assessments of her power and beauty, even my attraction to her. After all, Petrichor saved my life.

Having gotten a glimpse of the memories of my performance before the High Council, including my memory of smashing Aldor's nose, Stella showed a surprising interest in my legal knowledge. So, I downloaded every bit that I had. I also freely shared most of my family history, and she laughed at the many memories concerning my most mischievous brother, the Ginger. She was also fascinated by my memories of my sister, Bonnie, and accepted without question, how her partner, Tessa, fit into her rapidly expanding family tree. She could not wait to meet them. I could not wait to make it happen.

At the end of each day, Stella came to me to share what she had learned from the others.

Stella loved her time with Helen and Bobbi. Helen stepped up to share stories of women in the human world of business and enterprise – as well as the Tao of her Uncle Gus. Bobbi shared her connections between the conjoined worlds of energy and magic, and the thin veil between life and death, with the promise of passing on the esoteric secrets handed down from the women in her own blood line when Stella was ready. Eddie taught Stella how to cook, while Stella surreptitiously downloaded everything there was to know about his military skills and background. She did not understand why humans had to go to war with each other, but she appeared fascinated over the way it could be carried out.

Michelle turned into the unlikeliest Mary Poppins. When Gina needed time to feed and soothe Apollo, Michelle was there to whisk Stella away to explore, teach and bond. Michelle shared stories of her life on Centauri and on earth. When the information Michelle was sharing was purely educational, she did it digitally in a download, but when Michelle was sharing her emotional development from her time here on earth, she did it aurally, with words, so that the fine nuances would not be lost in translation. Stella, in turn, shared her own limited experiences of life on Centauri with Michelle, striking a happy balance transmitting that information telepathically, but in English, not numbers.

While Stella could not fully explain to Michelle how she was able to save her brother the morning of his birth, she was able to recreate the physical process of generating the energy from her hands at will. Michelle made Stella promise not to do this outside of the collective home, which now had expanded to incorporate Michelle and Everett's property as well.

Everett taught Stella everything there was to know about Jayney. On clear, moonless nights he would take Stella out for some joy rides among the planets in our solar system, letting her take the controls for short periods in open space while he stood behind her, guiding her hands along the control panel.

Whitey took Stella for hikes through the mountains and woods, explaining from his wolf's eye view the flora and fauna of the area, and the hierarchies of both. And while he never physically transformed in front of her, he allowed her to observe the process through a visit to his mind.

Lenny loved to play Toro the bull with Stella, holding his long index fingers on both sides of his head while he stooped over, pawed the ground with his feet and then charged her. Stella, giggling and shrieking, dematerialized only to reappear after he had passed.

Even Eileen pitched in, providing Stella with access to Eileen's wealth of knowledge of both human and animal anatomy and physiology, and the many curative ways to treat both.

Once Gina explained to the human legacy of the group, Scarlett, Savanna and Lucian, that Stella was my daughter from another mother, they treated her like the sister she was. As the pandemic restrictions loosened, they would come by to babysit, take her for walks in our estate area, watch children's movies and sing songs with her. They even played dress-up. Lucian loved not being the youngest member of the family of misfits. They did not care that Stella was from Centauri, after all, Michelle and Everett had rendered that concept comfortable to them and they seemed fine with the changes in Gina and me. They also did not fully understand the depth of Stella's knowledge and abilities, and she did nothing in their presence, or in public, to expose it, at least until that one time where it changed all of our lives, forever.

But out of all of the members of the group, it was Claire who excited Stella the most.

On the afternoon Apollo was born, I took Stella out to meet Claire. To everyone's surprise, Claire said, "C'mon little lady, climb on my back and let me take you for a ride."

Before Claire had finished her sentence, Stella was perched on Claire's withers, her legs tightly wrapped around the base of her neck and her hands grasping Claire's mane. Claire winked at me and slowly started to amble from the side paddock to the back property, where she broke into a cantor while Stella shrieked and laughed with delight. The normally ice queen Michelle, raced along beside them, circling Claire like a blur to make sure she would be there to catch Stella should she fall.

The ride became a morning ritual and, each evening, Stella loved to share her daily adventures with Claire with the rest of us when we sat down to eat dinner. Stella also would join Lucian out back with Claire whenever he came by to clear up the stables and helped Eddie whenever he stopped over to groom the mule. Claire was no longer just my therapy animal and confident. She shared her wisdom with us all.

Claire even conjured up Mr. Rogers in Stella's presence, and much to Michelle's chagrin, would take the child on tandem rides with her holographic beau through the darkness of the back property. Stella shared that Mr. Rogers like to nuzzle her, which made the hair on her head stand on end from a static charge.

"You have been blessed, Jimmy." Claire said to me as I sat on a bucket in her barn sipping coffee in the middle of that night following the arrival of both children. "We all have been."

CHAPTER NINETEEN
(Apollo Rises)

While most of the family members focused on the more developed Stella, Gina's focus remained on Apollo. The good news was, like human infants, he needed his sleep to grow. The bad news was, like Centaurians, he grew more rapidly than a human child. This meant that he was always hungry, so that most of his waking hours found him attached to one or the other of Gina's breasts. Helen and Bobbi stayed on with us to lend a hand. Helen made sure that Gina kept up her own nourishment and Bobbi stepped in to take Apollo long enough to give Gina some short, but badly needed breaks. Gina made sure that she pumped enough extra bottles of breast milk to allow the others to handle a feeding or two.

Since I had nothing to measure it against, I was not sure how Apollo was developing. Within the first week he was responding to Gina's voice, focusing on her face, and tracking the movement of others who entered the room. Whenever Stella came in for a visit, he would smile at his sister and coo. He was fascinated with his hands and feet, which seemed to be in constant motion. By the third week he could hold his head up straight, was reaching for dangling objects and loved the sounds of the rattles he now grasped and shook. By the end of the first month, he was rolling over on his own and could sit up with one of us supporting him. Eileen was amazed each time she stopped by to check on his progress.

And Apollo was absorbing the thoughts and memories of everyone with whom he came into contact and was making complex associations among those people. Given the sources of his information, it was all relayed to me in English. Whenever I looked into his mind, I saw not only my own lifted thoughts and memories being streamed, but also those of Gina, Stella and even Claire. If, during those times that I engaged him, I thought about Helen, then streams of her, Bobbi, and Eddie's thoughts, all jumbled together, flowed through his mind. The same process followed if he thought of either Michelle or Everett – the other Centauri's thoughts were also incorporated. Oddly, Apollo seemed to lump the thoughts of Eileen, Lenny, and Whitey together, trying to make order out of those free radicals.

But it was during his second month that Apollo started flexing his muscles. The first time we really noticed it was when Gina had placed him in his crib to go down for a nap, and then joined some of the crew in the dining room for some lunch. Stella and Lucian were out in the back with Claire.

Even though we had the infallible advantage of having numerous people being able to keep a close eye on the sleeping child telepathically, the humans in the group, including Eileen, Lenny, Helen and the two young ladies, insisted that we also employ the good old fashioned video baby monitor so that everyone could share in the responsibilities. When Apollo woke up, we paid him no mind as he rolled around on his back and began to babble, not having quite mastered vocalizing his thoughts. Then he lifted himself into a sitting position and maintained his balance while he gazed around the room.

"That child is doing what human babies, six-months-old, cannot do," Eileen offered.

Apollo pulled himself up on the railings and continued to babble with more intensity as he scanned the room, fixing on the small teddy bear that was resting on the pillows on his parents' bed.

Apollo then pointed towards the teddy bear, babbled a bit more, and with renewed concentration, blurted the word "bear," and the stuffed toy lifted from its resting spot and floated across the room and into the child's outstretched hands. The child crushed the bear with a hug and dropped back down to a sitting position, giggling hysterically.

"That child is doing what no other Centaurian I've ever heard of can do, no matter what age." Michelle commented with just a hint of pride.

* * * * *

By five months of age, Apollo was the size of an eighteen-month-old human, was able to walk and could speak and think in simple sentences. He also became Stella's sidekick, and his sister became Gina's favorite little helper with regards to anything Apollo. Indeed, it was Stella, who now looked like a five-year-old, who taught Apollo how to transport.

One late morning in early August, Gina and I were alone in the house, sitting on the back deck with Stella and Blue, who had become Stella's inseparable companion. Apollo was napping for shorter periods, and this time we all felt him reaching out telepathically for us as he awoke. Before either Gina or I could respond, Stella disappeared and a moment later materialized embracing Apollo in a bear hug. The boy had the same expression he had the first time he tasted vanilla ice cream, pure ecstasy.

"Again!" he shouted with delight. Stella obliged, this time transporting him right inside the glass doors of the living room, where we could still see them from our chaise lounges. Before Gina could stop them, Apollo shouted "Again!" and they disappeared for a third time, this time reappearing down in the yard, directly beside Claire, who was sampling some loose tree bark off a dying scrub oak tree. The three were then joined by Blue, who made her way down off the side deck the old-fashioned way, racing along the side of the house. Before Apollo could call for his next encore, I transported down and snatched both children up in my arms and returned with them to the chaise lounge on the deck, where Gina then cradled the boy and transported him into her room for a feeding while I distracted his sister by being an almost human tickle monster. I was glad she got my tickle genes.

Once she had been properly distracted by tickling to the point of breathlessness, I gave her a moment to calm down, and then explained to Stella how she needed to be careful when teaching her brother any of her tricks, until we had a better understanding of Apollo's gifts. We did not want him disappearing on his own to who knows where.

Don't worry daddy, Stella explained in her old soul mental voice, *I'm never going to let anything bad happen to Apollo.*

That's good, I responded in the same telepathic fashion, *because I'm never going to let anything bad happen to you.*

I had no idea how soon both promises would be tested.

CHAPTER TWENTY
(Internet Stars)

The COVID-19 Pandemic had raced across the globe throughout the spring and summer of 2020, indiscriminately taking lives, overburdening health care systems, closing schools, destroying businesses, and generally crushing economies. Most of humanity was misinformed about the lethality of the virus by the bad information they were getting from the biased media outlets and therefore frightened about what they did not understand. Deaths from all the other major indicators like flu, heart disease, diabetes and even cancer seemed to plummet because every passing was now attributed to the new virus.

Given the novelty of this virus, the clueless federal and local governments had played a mostly reactionary game, until the President made a bold move and threw the entire resources of the government behind the pharmaceutical industry for an unprecedented rapid development of a vaccine. But, given that this was an election year, there were ulterior political motives at play which intentionally delayed that process, and kept the government's heel on the throat of its populace through mandatory shutdowns, lock-ins, social distancing, and mask mandates. This ultimately led to a breakdown in the social fabric with the intent by a cabal of professional, globalist politicians to cause a complete reset of what our country, and the world around us, would be in the future.

And I could not give a rat's ass about any of it. Instead, I capitalized on the insanity and made millions investing in related pharmaceutical stock and those pipeline industries that were necessary to bring the vaccine to market. If the rest of humanity wanted to eat the pablum being offered by the powers that be, let them. As long as my family of misfits got what they needed when they needed it, I was happy. I was sure the "families" I had left behind on the East Coast were making an even bigger killing, in all understandings of that word.

I was not a complete asshole. I made significant anonymous donations to local groups and charities set up to aid and provide relief to the economically impacted. I also supported any of the local businesses in my Berthoud and surrounding communities that put up a fight, particularly those that showed the balls to stand up to government tyranny. But they were few and far between. Members of our local community had been reduced to either complete capitulation or defiantly conducting their business like the speakeasies of prohibition. In response, as with all sinking ships, the rats rose to the upper deck of even this rural community, and you now found neighbors informing on each other. Misery loves company.

But true charity begins at home, so, earlier that summer, I convinced Helen, Bobbi, Eddie, and Whitey to use the time that The Oracle remained shuttered by government edict to work together and perform a complete renovation, which I would fund.

In this way, we also could keep some of the local tradesmen busy and their suppliers with an income stream. We hired a local architect and engineering firm and spared no expense on the design, or the materials used in the project, which began on Monday, August 3, 2020. On the day the work began, we rented three luxury RVs to house the displaced occupants, including the Sirens, and parked them on the back of Helen's property.

I, in turn, kept myself busy renovating the east wing of the first floor to convert the space that was once the Master Bedroom, *en suite* and Birthing room into two equal-sized, large bedrooms with a newly configured Jack-n-Jill bathroom suite between them. Gina and the two children stayed with Michelle, while Everett and I, working around the clock at Centaurian speed, completed the project in one week. We might have done it faster, but Everett was not as handy with a skill saw as he was with a Hadron Distributor. The project was a pleasant distraction and it felt good swinging a hammer again.

By September, Helen and Bobbi were excited to show me the progress on The Oracle, beyond a telepathic peek through their own perception, so we planned for an on-site visit so they could give me the walk through. We chose Friday, September 11th, because the misguided mayor of New York City had decided to gut the annual sacred commemoration of the heroes of 9-11, which I had observed on television each year since 2002, so I needed a distraction away from my house. Gina thought it would be good for the children to visit with Helen and Bobbi, so we decided to make it a family trip. We could have just materialized at their location, but Gina thought that the scenery and fresh air might do us all good. At eight a.m., we packed the two children into their safety seats in the back of the Toyota RAV 4, and off we went.

Colorado had recently relaxed its COVID mandate to allow the limited opening of some of its non-essential businesses, so there was a surprising number of vehicles on the two laned County Road 23E heading in the general direction of Longmont and Hygiene. The traffic continued to move smoothly as the road converted to North 83rd Street but started to slow a mile or so later just south of Yellowstone Road. By the time we reached the crest of the hill leading to and overlooking Woodland Road, which would take us the rest of the way into Hygiene, for the first time since I had come to Colorado, traffic came to a complete standstill. I felt like I was back on the West Side Highway in New York on a Friday afternoon.

Our hilltop vantage point provided us with a birds-eye view of the reason. The fence of the large cattle ranch on the northern corner where the two roads met had been knocked down and a herd of cattle had exited the property and spilled out onto the roadway. Unfortunately, a young calf had been struck by the lead motor vehicle and now lay prone and wounded on the roadway, with its mother and other concerned herd members circling protectively around it. People had exited the first few cars and were trying to drive some of the cattle back through the fence line to clear the roadway. I could hear the sounds of emergency vehicles approaching from the distance. I was about to turn around and head back in search for an alternative route, when Gina shouted, "Stella, no!"

Before I could do anything, Stella had disappeared. I looked into her mind to see where she was going, and the first image that presented was an up-close view of the face of the crying injured calf. I gazed down the hill and saw Stella materialize within the circle of cattle besides the downed baby bovine. I threw the car in park, and not trying to draw any further attention, pulled up the hoody on my sweatshirt and raced down the hill with athletic human speed. As I arrived outside the cattle circle I could see everyone standing around with their iPhone cameras focused on its center.

Stella's hands were again emitting that bright white light as she stood over the crying calf, running her hands along its injured and bloody body. As the world watched, the calf's wounds healed under the white glow that covered it, and after a moment, the tiny animal rose hesitantly to its feet and cried out anxiously just as its mother arrived at its side. I had no choice but to transport past the circle of protective cattle and, arriving in its center, in the blink of an eye, snatched Stella up in my arms and disappeared. We materialized back in the front seat of my car, Stella on my lap, just as the local fire company, siren blasting, passed us going the wrong way on the oncoming side of the roadway. I handed Stella to Gina, made a rapid U-turn, and headed back towards home driving as fast as I could without drawing any more attention to our vehicle.

My heart had not raced like this since the night of the Storm. The whole ride back, while Gina tried to calm the confused and frightened children, all I could think of was *what do I do now?*

CHAPTER TWENTY-ONE
(Getting Your Head Straight)

My father, who had boxed during his time in the Navy, had taught us all, including Bonnie, from the time we were very young that if you ever find yourself in a physical altercation, your first blow should be to your opponent's nose. There was a method to his madness. You do not have to be strong to be effective. The strike immediately causes the membranes within their nasal passages to swell, which reduces the oxygen flow at a time where their body is already burning through it quicker than normal. It causes the recipient's eyes to tear, which makes it harder to see their opponent. All of the closely positioned nerve endings in the nose makes for a short trip to the brain, and instantly causes confusion. And finally, if your opponent is a bleeder, the blood that passes out the front of their nose invokes fear that you have done them serious damage, which gives you a psychological advantage, and the blood flowing into their throat causes a choking sensation and makes it even harder to meet the already taxed oxygen requirements. Citizen Aldor learned all of this during Everett's hearing before the High Council on Proxima-b.

At this moment I felt like the Universe had just landed a square shot on my proboscis.

I just wanted to get my family back home before something else bad happened. I felt a growing frustration that travelling slowly by car past the extending line of oncoming vehicles idling in place, due to the stampede behind me, was not doing us any favors. Just as I passed the last of those cars, I felt that same galvanization I had last experienced on Centauri, which caused me to tap on the brakes, and the next thing I knew, the Toyota and its occupants were in my garage.

I threw the car into park, killed the engine, and looked over at Gina.

That wasn't me.

I reached out to Stella.

No Daddy. I didn't do it. Stella pointed towards her brother in the back seat.

When I turned to face Apollo, he was sitting safely in his car seat, eyes closed, with his right hand firmly grasping the passenger side door handle. At that moment, his eyes popped open, and he smiled.

"I did it, I did it," he cackled. "Weee!"

By the time I had ushered the family out of the car and into the house, Everett and Michelle were sitting at the dining room table with Everett's Razer Pro 17 laptop open and running.

Stella is already all over the Internet. Michelle transmitted.

Everett simultaneously downloaded the twelve different YouTube videos opening on his multiscreen all capturing some or all of Stella's come-to-Jesus moment. Fortunately, there was only one video capturing me running down the roadway and into the gathering crowd. It was taken from behind me from one of the cars parked on the hill immediately before my own and, as I had my hoody pulled up, did not show my face. Once I merged with the crowd, it did not clearly capture my transportation. Thank God for small miracles.

But the rest of those videos caught various viewpoints of the main event. The macabre human crowd had all been filming this badly injured calf, crying for its mother, while the rest of the cattle formed a protective circle around it in defiance of the other more compassionate people's attempt to shoo them out of the roadway and back onto the ranch property.

Suddenly, a young girl in a pink, My Pony jacket, with a thick mane of burgundy hair, appeared out of nowhere beside the injured calf in the center of the cattle circle. Because she was kneeling and hunched over the animal, and the large bovines surrounding her obscured a lot of the viewpoint, there were no direct videos of her face, but the good stuff was all captured by the cameras. Her hands began to glow with that luminous white light, which seemed to extend and then congeal around the very nasty wound in the calf's torso. And then, like magic the light disappeared, and the young animal's side was as pristine as the day it was calved. One video was so clear I could read the calf's RFID ear-tag:

911. I could also make out a small red logo *Cowsensor* on the tag. As the calf raised itself onto shaky legs, its mother appeared in the camera shots and further obscured Stella right at the time I snatched her, which emerged on the screen as a brief flash of the navy color of my sweatshirt as we both disappeared, to the spontaneous soundtrack of surprised WTFs.

The videos already had steadily rising numbers of thousands of views and the comments all referred to Stella as the mysterious "Pink Pony Girl," with various commentary describing her as being everything from an elf, alien, and even a tiny witch.

It gets worse. Michelle transmitted. *It's been picked up by the Associated Press.*

Everett pulled up the AP webpage on his laptop which displayed under its "Top Stories" banner the headline "Pink Pony Girl Miracle" over a culled together stream of a number of the videos, and a brief printed description of their contents. The only good thing in the story was that the rancher had been quoted as stating that the miracle calf and its mother would be spared being sold or slaughtered.

The Wilbur effect, Everett shared. I never knew he was a Charlotte's Web fan.

Suddenly Claire's sultry voice entered my head. I had left the toilet seat up again.

Go and lay low at Bonnie's. I've just given her the heads up. She'll meet you at the Salisbury Country House.

"We'll take care of everything here and tell the others." Michelle said, as comforting as the moment would allow.

Everett nodded in agreement. "I'll keep you posted."

Sometimes you can't overthink it, you just have to act.

I grabbed Stella and Gina grabbed Apollo, and Gina and I clasped hands. Then darkness.

CHAPTER TWENTY-TWO
(Salisbury Redux)

We appeared *en mass,* still clutching each other, in the center of the great walled in garden in the back of Bonnie and Tessa's country estate. It was mid-afternoon, and the grounds looked exactly as it had on my first trip almost two years before, even the croquet balls were just where I remembered them.

This place is beautiful, Gina shared.

Apollo, whose face was buried in Gina's chest, slowly lifted his head and scanned the area. Stella squirmed out of my grasp and then transported to where the red croquet ball lay. She was about to pick it up, when we heard the back door to the manor house slide open.

"Don't be screwing with those balls, young lady," sounded so unusual when shouted with the posh, BBC News, British accent of my sister's spouse, the Baroness Tessa De Mille, of the House of Tudor.

Tessa was followed out the door by my sister, who was wearing a white kitchen apron with the words, 'Kiss The Cook' in bright red letters across its center.

"Welcome family!" Bonnie shouted, in her affected, slightly less posh British accent. "Come children and give your Aunties a hug."

"Should we be masking?" Tessa asked Bonnie as she reached for the cloth mask sticking out of her front pocket.

"No, sweetie," Bonnie replied, "they're all Centaurian hybrids, they don't carry viruses."

The children both accessed and downloaded my memories of my sister and Tessa, then simultaneously materialized at their feet, embracing both women with unexpected gusto.

"What do you feed these children?" Tessa gasped as Apollo hugged her around her thighs.

"Easy now, Apollo" Gina called to him. "Must not break Aunty Tessa."

What a beautiful, young lady! Bonnie shared telepathically, as she reached down and lifted Stella into her arms. Even her thoughts sounded posh.

My daddy is your brother, like Apollo is mine. Stella responded, expressing her understanding of their connection.

"That's right," Bonnie said, shifting to aural communication so as not to offend her telepathically challenged spouse. "You are as bright as a penny!"

"From now on children, we are all going to speak our thoughts around Aunty Tessa." Gina proclaimed, as we closed the distance in human speed.

Stella hopped out of Bonnie's arms and freed Tessa from Apollo's embrace.

"Come here, handsome." Bonnie called to the unmoored boy as Stella offered Tessa a much more comfortable hug. Stella was already up to Tessa's waist. Apollo transported into Bonnie's arms.

"Easy there, killer," Bonnie gasped, slipping into traces of her Bronx accent.

Apollo relaxed his grip and leaned back to get a better look at his Aunty. Bonnie performed her own assessment of the boy and tousled his hair.

"Oof, I see the Ginger gene rises," Bonnie said with a laugh, looking over at Stella. "You'll need to watch these two."

Suddenly, I was distracted by the sound of soft fluttering wings around my ears.

"ABC?"

The chirping confirmed my guess, as my three Sprites appeared hovering in formation before me. I held out my hand to allow them to land. Suddenly, Apollo materialized in my free arm, his eyes glued in fascination to the tiny beings. I tossed them into the air, and they performed some aerial acrobatics as they buzzed around his head. When Alieki landed on his nose for a second, Apollo went a bit cross-eyed trying to follow her, and broke into a large smile.

"Come on, let's get you settled in your rooms," Tessa said, turning back towards the house, "Bonnie has dinner on. You can bring us up to speed over Tea."

CHAPTER TWENTY-THREE
(A Quick Catch Up)

We had learned from Michelle that Centauri babies needed to sleep like their human counterparts because of their accelerated growth, so even if Gina and I did not need to sleep much, the children's sleeping gave us breaks to do whatever else was needed without the distraction. Apollo's enhanced growth led to his being weaned from the breast over the past month with the early appearance of his teeth. He was now eating solids, which basically meant just tossing whatever vegetable dish I was eating into a blender or allowing him to chew softer foods, like mashed potatoes, boiled vegetables and breads and pastries. Bonnie's vegetarian spread worked out perfectly for all of us.

After a nice meal, Gina put the children down for the night together in a queen-sized bed in one of the guest rooms on the second floor. I had helped clear away the dinner plates and put them in a dishwasher that looked like it could perform hospital level sterilization. Tessa was brewing some coffee in a French Press while Bonnie put out four servings of English Trifle by the time Gina returned. Gina's spontaneous materialization almost caused Tessa to drop the glass coffee carafe.

"New house rules," Tessa declared. "No popping in and out. And that goes for the kids too."

"When in Rome, as they say," Bonnie added, "we must appear at all times completely human."

"Agreed." Gina responded, contritely. I nodded in accord.

We don't want to give poor T a coronary. Bonnie shared telepathically.

"The world has gone mad over this COVID virus," Tessa complained as she played mother and poured the coffee. "Neighbors are watching neighbors here like the Vichy French. We all must be extra careful not to give anyone a reason to look twice at you or the kids. The whole thing is doing my head in."

"Happily," Bonnie said, "despite the brief appearance on the AP website, there's been no mention of the Pink Pony Girl story by the BBC, ITV or Channel 4."

"Hopefully," Tessa added, "those internet videos will run their course and be relegated to Big Foot territory."

"Until then," Bonnie said, "you are welcome to stay here as long as you like."

"But you may want to think about dying Stella's hair," Tessa added. "It's a rather unique color, and clear as day in those videos Bonnie showed me."

"Sounds like a plan," Gina responded.

"I can pick some hair coloring up on my next trip into town," Tessa volunteered. "Something more your color, Gina."

"I'll come with you," Gina offered.

"Sure, but you'll have to mask up." Tessa replied. "Some of the locals go out of their way to complain to the Salisbury council about public safety outliers."

"A mask is probably a good thing, giving our reason for being here." Gina agreed.

"So, brother, Claire gave me the broad strokes about what happened," Bonnie pivoted, "would you like to fill us in on the details?'

I finished my serving of trifle and went for a second helping of both dessert and coffee. I was surprisingly famished. When I returned to the table I recounted the events as they occurred, between bites, in as much detail as I could remember, and Gina added what additional facts she could see from her broader viewpoint in the car, which went far beyond my adrenaline-fueled tunnel vision operating in the moment.

As I finished my narrative, I made a mental note to tell Everett to get rid of the car.

Already taken care of, Everett interjected out of the ether. *Whitey has removed the plates and the vin numbers and is dumping it into the deepest end of Crater Lake at this very moment. Eddie is house sitting at your place for the duration and, with Lucian's help, will be caring for Claire. Lenny has Blue at his place, and Michele has already hacked the DMV and has scrubbed all records of ownership of the Toyota.*

Just sit tight, Jimmy. Claire then chimed in. *We got this. Love to Gina and the babies. Claire out!*

Bonnie laughed. "Just got to love a telepathic party line."

She then recounted the shared information to Tessa.

"It must be madness in that head of yours, Jimmy Moran." Tessa cried in wonder.

"Only when he leaves the toilet seat up," Gina said, laughing, as Bonnie joined in. Tessa shook her head but smiled as she surrendered to the happy mood of the other women.

I was not sure whether it was just the vestiges of the human part of me responding to a very long and stressful day, or whether transporting four beings across the pond took more energy than I expected, but, despite the sugar rush and caffeine top off, I felt physically exhausted in a way I had not felt since I was brought back from the dead.

Are you okay? Gina asked.

Why don't you lay down for a kip, Bonnie added. *You too, Gina.*

I was about to dematerialize from kitchen to the bedroom when I remembered Tessa's admonition.

When in Rome, Gina shared, as she took my hand and led me human style out of the room.

CHAPTER TWENTY-FOUR
(Brunette's Have More Fun)

While I slept deeply, I did not sleep well. I dreamt that I was back standing before the Centauri High Council, but it had nothing to do with defending Everett. I was being called to account for failing to protect Interstellar. Petrichor sat in her center balcony looking frightened. Aldor was pointing his accusing finger in my direction. *This is all his fault!*

01001110 01101111 01110100 01101000 01101001 01101110
01100111 00100000 01101101 01110101 01110011 01110100
00100000 01101000 01100001 01110000 01110000 01100101
01101110 00100000 01110100 01101111 00100000 01101111
01110101 01110010 00100000 01100100 01100001 01110101
01100111 01101000 01110100 01100101 01110010 00101100
00100000 01001010 01101001 01101101 01101101 01111001
00100000 01001101 01101111 01110010 01100001 01101110
00101110

Nothing must happen to our daughter, Jimmy Moran.

The very real sound of Petrichor's voice in my head woke me with a start and caused me to bolt upright in bed. I was disoriented. The sun had already risen and was peeking under the bottom of blackout curtains. Gina was nowhere to be found. I transported into the children's room and found it empty as well.

I was about to transport to the kitchen when I remembered Tessa's proclamation. We were in a no-fly zone.

I tried to scan the area for a sense of the children's mental presence but there was nothing. Then I reached out telepathically for Gina and Bonnie and came up empty.

I did not hear a car pull up until the sounds of car doors slamming drew my attention to the front of the house. I transported to the front window and lifted the shade. Gina and Tessa were laughing as they removed some packages from the backseat of Tessa's brand new but unnaturally silent 2021 Jaguar I-Pace all-electric crossover. Bonnie and the children were nowhere to be found.

Where are the children?

Gina glanced up at my window.

With Bonnie. She replied.

No one else is here. I replied with as much excitement as my thoughts could generate. *Scan for yourself.*

Tessa, who was oblivious to our telepathic conversation, entered the front door and called out.

"We're home!"

I met Tessa in the front hallway, having descended the stairs four at a time in an attempt to comply with her mandate, and she immediately handed me her packages. "Oh, thank God," she said as she relinquished them, "Those are heavy. Could you be a dear and take them into the kitchen for me?"

As soon as she turned back towards the front door, I took advantage of the opportunity to transport to and from the kitchen, leaving the packages on the large center island right opposite the refrigerator. I was back before Tessa had ushered Gina safely through the doorway.

"Here, Jimmy, take those from Gina," Tessa instructed, obviously not comprehending that, as a result of our Tellurian-Centaurian hybridization, Gina was probably stronger than me, and I was stronger than any human on earth. I did as I was told, this time slow walking them to the same counter space.

Daddy, daddy, we saw the fairies!

Apollo materialized in my arms pointing in the direction of the oversized patch of tall shrubbery in the distance by the back garden wall. I saw Bonnie standing on the outer edge of the shrubbery holding open an exit row in its center just as Stella exited. But she was not actually touching the bushes, she just held her hand by its opening. I remembered my own time in Bonnie's Neverland during my last visit here.

"Now Apollo," Gina said half-heartedly as she lifted the child from my grasp into her own, "what did we tell you about transporting while we're here in your Aunties' house?"

Gina turned with the child in her arms to Tessa to make sure she was paying attention.

"No transporting." Apollo sighed, his excitement from a moment ago quickly dissipated.

I reached out telepathically to Stella, who was slowly approaching at human speed hand-in-hand with her Aunt Bonnie.

Why didn't you answer me? I asked.

When?

Just a little while ago.

I didn't hear you, daddy.

I'm so sorry, Jimmy. Bonnie chimed in. *That place is a telepathic dead zone, nothing gets in or out of there without the fairies' permission.*

No worries, I conveyed to reduce the tension, *just glad you're safe.*

"There you are," Tessa shouted at Stella though the doorway, "come on in here child and let Aunty T give you a mini-makeover."

Stella released Bonnie's hand and teleported to inside the kitchen between Tessa and Gina.

How come she can do it? Apollo asked all that could receive him as he wiggled out of Gina's arms and ran over to Bonnie just as she came through the door.

Because life is just not fair, little man. Bonnie responded as she tousled the young boy's hair. *But why don't we balance that out with a delicious ice cream cone?* she added, grabbing his hand and leading him to the freezer.

Gina downloaded the haircoloring process to Stella while she aurally reminded her of Tessa's no transporting rule. Stella beamed.

The little girl pointed at the model on the *eSalon* hair kit Tessa was holding and then at Gina's hair.

"We'll be twins!" Stella shouted.

"Good as!" Tessa added. "Let's go to my *en suite* sweetie. Your hair isn't going to color itself."

Stella looked back at Gina.

Are you coming? She asked telepathically.

Wouldn't miss it for the world! Gina responded, taking the child's hand, as the two followed Tessa out of the kitchen.

Daddy, the elf king winked at me! Apollo said.

CHAPTER TWENTY-FIVE
(Suspicious Strangers)

Why is it that women are intrepid in taking on challenges that could end badly? Those challenges range from something as simple as coloring their own hair to something as harrowing as marrying the wrong man. Whatever drives them, one of the great things about the female sex, and that list is endless, is their willingness to take what they learn from their personal experience and share it among the sisterhood. In the case of Tessa, Gina and Stella, their sharing of the concept of hair coloring, vital here among humans, had just gone intergalactic. The potential repercussions to the permanently blond Centauri race were unfathomable.

The hour I waited to observe the outcome of their cosmetological endeavor was spent having coffee with my sister while Apollo played tag with my ABC Sprites close by in the garden. Bonnie had given him a special dispensation concerning the no-fly rule so that he stood a fair chance against the three wily Sprites in the contest, as long as he promised not to transport beyond the surrounding walls or try to enter the fairy vegetation on his own.

I could feel the unqualified love Bonnie and Tessa had for my children, as my sister and I watched in silence while the giggling Apollo popped from behind one perimeter tree to another as he tried to avoid the relentless Sprites.

When her time comes, Stella should have Nana's talents as well, Bonnie shared proudly. *There's magic in her blood that even surpasses her amazing evolutionary gifts.*

I entered Bonnie's mind and she showed me how the otherwise impenetrable vegetation that protected the fairies at the back of her garden had opened voluntarily for my daughter earlier that morning without Bonnie's intercession. Unfortunately, the Nana trait stayed true to its feminine bloodline, as Bonnie then showed me a frustrated Apollo unsuccessfully attempting to make his own way into the bushes. He could not even transport inside the magically protected foliage. Each time he just vibrated wildly for a moment before being firmly planted on his butt, a bit dazed, in the same spot he started. In the contest between magic versus science, the older sorcery won.

Jimmy? I could suddenly hear Claire's sultry voice in my head. Given that I was still in Bonnie's mind, she heard it too.

We are sorry to pop in like this, but Whitey has something to report.

Yeah, Jimmy, I recognized Whitey's distinct timbre, *I was just in Berthoud grabbing some coffee at Grandpa's Cafe with Nick and Billy from my work crew before we headed off to finish up on The Oracle job. I overheard one of the locals, Carl, talking at his regular table of retirees about how a couple of strangers stopped by Side Tracked last night showing an iPhone close-up of the little girl, lifted from the calf video, to the patrons there.*

Did you get a description of these guys? I asked.

Sorry Jimmy, I can communicate telepathically with the gifted, but I don't have your ability to just read someone's mind. The connection has to be open on both ends, like this. Carl is a bright guy – I think he is a physicist - but he's all human. I just heard what I heard.

Hold on a sec, Claire chimed, *I just checked Whitey's memory, and there was something about Carl mentioning that the two guys were 'too well dressed to be government types.'*

Okay, Whitey chimed back in, *Lenny just arrived at your house and is talking with Eddie out front. They are both carrying long guns in from Lenny's SUV.*

Okay, Jimmy, we gotta go, Claire shared. *Everett and Michelle just arrived. We'll have to get back to you.*

And just like that, the party line went silent.

CHAPTER TWENTY-SIX
(Coming Full Circle)

"Aunty T is taking us to see Stonehenge!" Stella whooped as she circled around the garden table at a dizzying speed that was just shy of full-on transporting. Worried that she was about to create a tornado, I gathered the coffee cups and plates to a spot right before me and leaned over them so they would not lift off the table from the vacuum forming around us. Bonnie held tight to the opposite edge of the table.

What's Stonehenge? Apollo's thoughts arrived from his hiding spot behind a large Field Maple tree along the side garden wall towards the back of the property.

Stella quickly downloaded everything about the ancient stone monument that she lifted from Tessa's brain into her brother's. When the now excited Apollo joined in on the race with his sister, the table itself started to lift from the draft.

Children, stop!

Gina appeared in the funnel and snatched the two urchins as they passed her, like a bear snatching salmon from a rushing stream. *Impressive all around.*

Stella's now matching brown locks were in complete disarray but gone was all hints of the ginger gene. Apollo stared from Gina's other arm at his sister's hair, and then extended a forelock of his own with his fingers to assess the difference.

I want hair like mommy's too! He declared telepathically.

"Maybe when we get back from our outing," Bonnie promised, just as Tessa arrived in the garden, "but first, let's make you two presentable!"

"There's no rush," Tessa replied. "Pulled some strings with my cousin, Geoffrey Chamberlain, who sits on the Board of English Heritage, and he's booked us all in for that 'Stone Circle Experience' today at six p.m. We'll have the run of the stones all to ourselves."

"One more reason I love her," Bonnie shouted as she led the children through the back door in search of a hairbrush, her Bronx accent on full display as she closed, "She's got connections up the wazu!"

* * * * *

The Stonehenge Shuttlebus arrived at Tessa's gate at five-fifteen p.m., sharp.

"You must tell Sir Geoffrey that we owe him big-time," Bonnie said to Tessa as we loaded the kids into the car seats along the back bench of the Shuttle. Bonnie then took the spot between the two children and Gina, Tessa and I slid into the middle bench. I felt a great deal calmer knowing my sister Bonnie "MaGoo" was not at the wheel of this vehicle. The last time she drove me to her country home in England, I almost shit myself.

The trip to the historical site was pleasantly uneventful. We were met at its main entrance by a dignified older female volunteer who introduced herself to the group as Branwen Matholwch, although if you paid me I could not repeat her last name back to her.

She's Welsh! Bonnie shared. *Their language makes Irish sound comprehensible.*

Once we had safely disembarked, Branwen counted heads, made sure we were all wearing our face masks, and typed something into the small phone-like object she carried with her. She then turned on her heels, shouted, "Keep up!" and then led us through a passage and into the stone circle, while beginning her spiel, "The stones here at Stonehenge are aligned on the midwinter sunset-midsummer sunrise solstitial axis. . . ."

Gina took Stella's hand and I held firmly onto Apollo's just in case he saw something that caught his fancy and bolted for it, and the group fell into step behind the woman. I immediately stopped listening to the history lesson and started feeling. The four-thousand-year-old energy within the circle was palpable, and I wondered whether all of the stories my grandmother, Bridey "Nana"

Burke, told us about her bloodline being descended from Druids were true. At that moment, Bonnie grabbed my free hand.

They were. Bonnie shared.

Stella came trotting over to us, took Bonnie's hand and led her towards what Branwen was describing the "Avenue" running directly outward from the passage below the central of three capstones, which Branwen identified as the "Summer Solstice" portal. The tour guide identified the "Heel Stone" on the Avenue in the distance and then turned towards the "Altar Stone," whose shadow, Branwen informed us, was a focus point of the Stonehenge monument during the midsummer weeks. Branwen then led us along the perimeter explaining the differences between the once whitish, now grey, monolithic sarsen stones and the smaller shaped blue stones.

I'm tired daddy, Apollo shared. I no sooner had lifted him up to my chest when he fell into a deep sleep with his face buried into my neck. He had continued to grow at his Centaurian rate, and was the size of a human toddler, so I was glad I had the Centaurian strength to carry him along for the remainder of the tour. I stopped to focus on a straight line of familiar-feeling letters carved about eye level into the interior face of one of the perimeter sarsen stones, and could also make out other, more faded, carvings that resembled daggers and axes. Tessa and Gina were ahead of me, having stayed close to Branwen from the outset, listening to everything she was sharing. Tessa because this was her homeland and she its ruling class. Gina because she always had been a history geek. I looked around for Stella and Bonnie, and thought I spotted them through the solstice portal standing beyond the circle down the Avenue by the Heel stone. The sun was well into its downward trajectory on the western horizon, leaving them both in shadowed silhouette on Stonehenge's eastern side. They were in deep conversation. When I reached out to get Stella's attention telepathically, I was blocked.

I reached out to Bonnie. *What are you and Stella doing by the Heel Stone?*

I'm not by the Heel Stone, Bonnie responded. *I'm over here with T and Gina.*

I looked over towards Branwen and confirmed what Bonnie had shared. Panicked, I turned back towards the Solstice corridor, but there was no one by the Heel Stone. Before I had the chance to do anything else, I felt Stella's hand take my free one.

Where have you been? I demanded telepathically.

Over there, Stella pointed through the solstice corridor.

"Okay," Branwen said as she came over to herd us out of the circle back through the portal we had entered, "that concludes our tour. If you have any questions you may ask me over the refreshments waiting for us in the visitor's center. Follow me."

Who were you talking to? I continued to press Stella as we walked behind the group.

She said she was your grandma, Stella said innocently, then skipped forward and took Bonnie's hand.

Nana always liked a big entrance, Bonnie shared, accepting Stella's hand without looking back at me.

In my confusion, I almost did not notice the huge images of the different Heritage volunteers and workers honored for their sacrifices during the pandemic through being projected onto the exteriors of the perimeter sarsen stones. The advanced technology employed in the effort drew a sharp line underscoring that we had just crossed back firmly into the twenty-first century and all of the problems that awaited us there.

CHAPTER TWENTY-SEVEN
(The Idyllic Life)

As the following weeks turned into months, I distracted myself playing old-school Lord of the Manor. Most of my alone time was spent reading through Tessa and Bonnie's Library full of first editions of the classic English literature I avoided during my formal education, beginning with the nine volumes of *The Life and Opinions of Tristram Shandy, Gentleman*, by Laurence Sterne. I read it slowly, not just to consume information, but to engage in the narrative experience. And I loved the character Uncle Toby and his constant references to his curious groin wound. I followed this up with a major dose of Dickens and then, for a different viewpoint, the Bronte sisters and finally Virginia Wolff. I came to realize that I wasted a lot of my youth watching television.

When we were really bored, Gina and I would sneak out during the night while the others slept and race along all the narrow country roads, stopping along the way to take in some of the manmade landmarks and natural beauty of this part of England. If it were still early enough, we would occasionally pop into some of the wonderful quaint pubs that could be found in any of the rural towns and sample their best local stouts, lagers, and ciders. Claire would have loved the names of these establishments, which usually involved some animal like a swan, pig, or lion, and would have particularly enjoyed the *The White Horse* at Quidhampton and *The Black Horse* in Hurdcott. Americans had the more personalized and far less creative tendency of naming their bars after themselves.

In the end, it felt a bit vampiric seeing England solely during nocturnal hours, but, as the locals say, needs must. I could not help wondering how many times during our excursions that Gina and I popped up and disappeared on digital video feed from the ubiquitous CCTV cameras in the British Government Communications Headquarters.

Tessa and Bonnie reengaged their collective sixty-plus years in academia and established a makeshift home-school for the children. At first, it was just something to keep everyone busy, but the women were amazed at how quickly the kids absorbed any and all information provided to them. There was to be no mind scavenging and downloading of information. The children had to learn information piecemeal at the speed and manner provided by their Aunties. No exceptions. Otherwise, their education would be complete through twelfth grade in an instant. And part of this construct was to fill our collective time in isolation.

Stella was the perfect teacher's pet, enjoyed the rules of order imposed by Tessa during class time and thrived over the added attention she received from Bonnie. Apollo, more of a follow your own rules savant, filched whatever Stella digested in class, and had to be constantly admonished not to disappear during class time so he could go play with the Sprites or unsuccessfully try to breach the fairy foliage on his own. On occasion, Apollo had to be reluctantly retrieved and returned to his desk in the Library by his dutiful sister. I was not sure in the end which of the two groups, Aunties, or children, enjoyed their mornings more.

Stella also received extra-curricular instruction on her "Nana legacy" from Bonnie. The two often disappeared for hours, first in the kingdom of the fairies in the garden, and then during day long trips with Bonnie to Grovely Wood, where the two shared thoughts while they silently walked the Roman Road, meditated by the Witches' trees, and visited with the larger, fairy enclaves that were found there. Both tutor and pupil blocked our telepathic delving beyond the scraps of information they chose to share with the rest of the family, usually with the closing comment, "a girl needs to have her secrets."

When all of the females went out for organized day trips to London for private shopping excursions in High Street establishments, negotiated and arranged by the ever politically connected and resourceful Tessa, Apollo and I spent our time playing a Centaurian adaptation of the "I Spy" game. We would start each round with "I spy, with my little mind" where the opponent, instead of naming the riddled item, transported to its location and either retrieved it or, if it were within eyesight, pointed to it. We made sure to always block the other's telepathic probing, given both of our willingness to cheat. If we really got bored, we donned our face coverings and went for long, one-way, human walks though the Salisbury countryside, ultimately finding a discreet spot and then transporting back to base camp once we had traveled as far as we wanted. We left a lot of curious sheep wondering where we had gotten off to.

And the children continued to grow, which was fine with the Aunties, because they loved nothing more than to continue to clothe their charges in the latest fashion upgrades from *Elfie London, Cath Kidson, Rachel Riley,* and *G.H. Hurt & Son.*

I received regular telepathic reports on what was happening back home from everyone who could transmit. Claire kept me up to date on what was happening at the homestead, and I was happy to hear that Scarlett and Savanna were spending a lot of time visiting her. Eddie of course was a permanent fixture and Lenny and Whitey regularly checked in on Claire and the property. As far as Claire could tell, the local hoopla about the Pink Pony Girl had died down, as people seemed more distracted by the tumultuous election which led to the United States government changing political leadership and basically, as Claire politely put it, continuing to go to shit. Government upheaval was a price I was willing to pay to protect my family.

England itself had fared no better given the appearance of a purportedly more virulent strain of COVID-19 developing right here in the Southern area of the country that fall, which led the Aunties to take extra precautions whenever they were compelled to venture out into the area, but behind our walls we were all healthy and happy.

Being that it was both children's first Christmas, despite the fact that it really had not snowed in the area since 2010, the Aunties pulled out all the stops, brought in decorators to create a Dickensian Holiday motif within the house, including a fifteen-foot Christmas tree. They spoiled us all with feast, fun, and gifts, which carried the family happily into the New Year. In the absence of public celebrations, 2021 arrived with a whimper, not a roar.

The new year continued on much like the old, and when the end of March arrived, the Aunties held a quiet birthday party for the kids, given that both first arrived on this planet on March 23rd, the year before. They were provided completely new wardrobes and shoes for every occasion. And while it was a bit indulgent, it was a necessity, given that in the six months we had been staying with them, the children had physically evolved so dramatically, that Stella was the size of a seven-year-old and Apollo looked just a year younger. And their mental development had advanced far beyond their physical. Despite limiting the daily classroom transmission of academic information to the human method, and barring its instantaneous download, both children were now effortlessly mastering advanced high school courses, including science and math. But the children were getting everything they needed and were being doted upon by their Aunties. They were safe, and that was all that mattered.

From all outward appearances, we were living a Henry James novel, and the idyllic life suited us just fine. But I knew it could not last forever. One of the few times I hated being right.

CHAPTER TWENTY-EIGHT
(When Home Calls)

Jimmy, you have to come home.

It was after midnight in Salisbury, on a late April night. I had gotten used to nocturnal silence during my family's stay with Bonnie and Tessa. I was in the middle of reading Virginia Wolff's *To the Lighthouse* when the telepathic message arrived. It had been so long since I heard Bobbi Angelini in my head, I did a mental double take.

What?

You need to come home. All of you. Bobbi repeated.

Is something wrong? I asked.

I don't know. She responded. *But Spirit says something big is going to happen and it must happen here. At your home. With the family.*

Bobbi had been my Berthoud family psychic-medium-witch since I was first introduced to her and her partner, Helen LaLousis, by Lenny when Gina and I first arrived in Colorado under the auspices of the federal government Witness Protection Program. Since that time, Bobbi had repeatedly demonstrated that she was the real deal and that you ignored her prognostications at your peril. Unlike her mediumship abilities, which provided clear communications from beyond the veil of specific facts and information, her predictions for the future, often provided to her by her Spirit Guide, were sometimes general. As she once explained to me, the future was malleable and prone to change by the decisions you made after the prediction. Her Spirit Guide had told her that one of our group was going to die the night of the Storm before a mafia hit team arrived at my home and put a bullet through my heart. And the Spirit Guide also predicted that I would not stay together with Gina, back when she was resolutely remaining in her human form. Once Michelle genetically converted Gina from a human to a Centauri hybrid like me, the future changed along with us.

But this was different. This was specific. I could not ignore it. I had to trust Bobbi for the good of my family.

Okay, I responded. *We're coming home.*

CHAPTER TWENTY-NINE
(And Back Again)

It's a funny thing, the future.

Bonnie poured herself a cup of Earl Grey and took a slice of toast from the chrome toast caddy then sat down at the long breakfast table in the kitchen where I had been ruminating all night since Bobbi's pop in.

I would never second-guess another psychic, given how I know first-hand that the information comes in shreds. Especially someone with Bobbi's gifts.

She blew on her cup to cool her tea and then took a sip.

And in all fairness, I knew you would all be leaving, sooner rather than later. Spaghetti was preparing me. I just did not want to face it head on.

Bonnie stared out through the glass sliding back doors at a pair of Magpies foraging crumbs from the plates on the garden table, where the children had eaten the strawberry pie T had baked for them the night before.

I love it here. I responded, gazing at the birds. *For the first time in a very long time, I haven't had to carry the weight of the world on my shoulders. You and T lifted that burden from me.*

In that one moment, our eyes met, and I experienced a vivid memory, an epiphany. We were children back in the Bronx. Bonnie was holding my hand, leading our family caravan in front of our siblings, one walking behind us, one in the pram and the last one still *in utero* while our very pregnant mother herded the family home from a day at McCoombs Park. I had just escaped certain death by a Mack truck on Jerome Avenue when I raced out before it in an attempt to save a scrum of pigeons that had gathered on the street. "Come Jimmy," Bonnie had whispered to me then, "you must stay alive, we have adventures to share."

T's going to be heartbroken. Bonnie mused, drawing me back to the moment, as she munched a corner of the toast and tossed the rest onto the plate before her. She took a measured sip of tea before switching to aural communication.

"She's grown quite fond of the children, you know."

"Who is 'she', the cat?" T grumbled as she entered the kitchen, crossed over to the pot of tea and rack of toast, and fixed herself a serving.

"We have to return to Berthoud." I yanked the band-aid off, sharing the bad news was the least I could do for Bonnie. Shoot the messenger.

"I know," T responded as she added a spoon of sugar to her tea, "Stella told me last night over pie. I've barely slept a wink all night."

* * * * *

We all gathered out in the garden. Gina and I had packed all of the children's clothes that would fit into the large knapsacks Bonnie and T had provided us.

"We were saving those for our trek through the Himalayas," T observed as she fastened a loose strap on the back of my knapsack, giving it a final tap for good measure. "This is a much more practical use for them."

I turned to face her and could see her lip was trembling.

"C'mon now T," I said, trying to keep things light, "where's that stiff upper lip you Brits are always bragging about?"

Her eyes started to tear, and she yanked me into a hug, in part, to hide her emotions from the children. "You take good care of them," T whispered into my ear, "or you'll have me to answer to."

Gina lifted Apollo to her hip. "We better get going."

Apollo transported into T's arms and almost knocked her off her feet in the process. As she recovered her balance she pulled him into a tight bearhug. She was weeping as he transported back into Gina's arms.

Bonnie escorted Stella, hand-in-hand, over to where I was standing. They were obviously communicating but had blocked me from listening in. As Bonnie offered me Stella's hand, the little girl shouted, "Wait!" and disappeared.

Bonnie continued her movement towards me and pulled me into a tight embrace.

We've shared some great adventures, haven't we, Jimmy?

I finally lost it and started to sob, right there on her shoulder. I was four years old again.

Why is Daddy crying? Apollo asked whoever could listen.

Bonnie grabbed my shoulders and separated us.

Spaghetti says it's all going to be fine. She shared.

"Man up, little brother," Bonnie said out loud.

I love you forever. She thought, pulling me close for one last kiss on my forehead.

Stella reappeared in that moment right next to Bonnie and me. She had a beautiful, thin gold chain around her neck, with a tiny diamond pendant hanging in her chest.

"I had to say goodbye to the fairies," she shared with us all. "The king gave me this!"

Stella lifted the pendant in her palm, and it sparkled brightly as it captured the early morning sun.

My three ABC Sprites appeared around Bonnie's head and Apollo shrieked in joy. Bonnie held out her hand and they alighted, then she walked over and slipped her hand into Apollo's sweater pocket. "You take care of the girls," Bonnie said as she gave him a peck on the cheek before pulling Gina into one final hug.

Bonnie then walked over and stood beside T, and the two women drew in deep breaths to regain control of their emotions.

"If you don't mind," Bonnie said. "We'd rather not watch you go, so please wait until we are out of sight before you disappear."

They then shared a glance and took one final look at us, and I at them, before they turned and resolutely walked hand-in-hand back towards the house.

I lifted Stella up onto my hip and reached over and took Gina's hand, then pictured home, and Claire. I felt my skin galvanizing and gazed off at the red croquet ball, sitting in that same place on the green lawn, and heard Apollo shout out, "I love you Aunties." Then blackness.

CHAPTER THIRTY
(Back in Oz)

When we materialized in the living room of our Berthoud home seconds later, we were not met with fanfare by the mayor and other dignitaries of munchkin land, but by Eddie, sleeping in one of the comfortable recliners in front of us while Food Network programs progressed on the giant flat screen television behind us. It was not our arrival that woke him, but the sound of Claire's trumpeting bray-nay coming from just outside in the backyard. The children dematerialized and in the next second we heard Claire's sultry voice shout, "Holy shit, what have they been feeding you two over in England?!"

"I must have dozed off," Eddie apologized as he rose from the chair, "Bobbi didn't say exactly when you'd be arriving."

Gina dropped her knapsack, walked over, and gave him a hug. "Thank you so much for taking care of the place while we were gone."

I had to give Eddie his due, the place was meticulous.

"I've prepared a simple garlic-veggie casserole for a late lunch," he said as Gina released him. He took a quick look around, grabbed his empty glass from the snack table and headed past us and into the kitchen, where he rinsed it and placed it into the dishwasher, "it's in the fridge. The oven has been pre-heating. Just toss it in on 250 and it will be ready in half an hour. There's a loaf of fresh bread in the closet."

"Why don't you stay and eat with us?" Gina asked as we followed him into that area.

"Thanks, but I better head back to The Oracle," he said, walking to the front hallway and picking up his Army duffel bag. "Bobbi mentioned a gathering here later tonight, so I'll probably see you back here then."

"See you tonight," I called after him as he headed out through the door. We watched as he followed his duffel bag into Helen's cherry red Mercedes, and then rolled out of the driveway.

I realized that Eddie had never asked me for anything since the day I met him. I made a mental note to deposit some serious cash into an account in his name.

We heard the sounds of children's laughter rising from the back yard and a moment later we spotted, through the sliding glass doors going out to the deck, Claire carrying our two kids bareback as she ambled through the side paddock and out into the back property. Stella held Apollo firmly between her arms extended before her, while she grasped Claire's mane firmly with both fists. The constant telepathic communication between the three of them confirmed their mutual enjoyment.

While it was much cooler in Berthoud than in Salisbury, April had been kind to Colorado. The snow had disappeared, its melt soaking into the earth. Perennial flowers and spring grass were sprouting everywhere.

By the time I deposited the two knapsacks in the children's rooms, Gina had already placed the casserole in the oven.

"As good as the food was over in England, I have missed Eddie's cooking so damn much," she said, inhaling the scent of garlic that quickly rose from the oven.

Welcome home strangers! Sounded the mental chorus, as Michelle and Everett appeared in our dining room. *Sorry to pop in but we felt your energy and just couldn't stay away.*

"What's on the menu?" Everett said, inhaling a lungful of garlic aroma.

"One of Eddie's casseroles," Gina said as she embraced Michelle in a hug that would maim a WWE wrestler.

"Plenty to go around." I offered, suddenly appreciating how much I had missed them both.

We've missed you guys too! Michelle responded.

Another toilet seat moment. *Will I ever learn?*

Count me in! Everett shared, as he materialized in a chair at the dining room table.

Incoming! Claire's sultry mental voice exclaimed, just as Apollo and Stella appeared in the living room.

Claire said we had to come in for lunch. Stella shared. "Aunty Michelle!" She shrieked and materialized in Michelle's embrace. I was pleased that Stella had extended the close familial title to our Centauri cousins, a common Irish application. Every older Irish couple that came to visit Spaghetti and Posey when we were growing up were introduced as "Aunt" and "Uncle" so-and-so and were instantly treated as blood family. And that meant that they fell into the 'ready to die for' category.

"Look at the size of you!" Michelle responded as she gave the young girl a slow human twirl before setting her down before her. "And what happened to your hair?"

While Stella shared her hair coloring experience, Apollo stood back shyly and stared at the Centaurians, searching his own memories for the connection. He had not yet developed the social cognizance of his sister when we had escaped to England. I downloaded enough information to make all of the proper connections, including that Everett had saved my life. Apollo smiled as he acclimated his thoughts, and in the next moment was sitting in Everett's lap, hugging him.

Over the next hour the six of us sat around the table sharing a wonderful meal, stories of our adventures in Salisbury, aurally so that no nuance would be lost, compelling laughter at many of the moments and sadness at the final parting. The meal reminded me of the many I experienced as a young child with my extended family back in the Bronx. It was transitional and cathartic and invoked an unexpected epiphany that my family had not been reduced over time, but now expanded across species, around the earth and throughout the universe. It even extended beyond the veil. We were all connected.

Afterwards, as Stella and Apollo performed an impromptu fashion show for Michelle of all of the British fineries the fairy godmothers had provided them, Gina handed me a large bowl containing the last of the garlic vegetables. *Claire is waiting.*

Everett took the bowl and transported with me down to the interior of Claire's Lair, where I was almost crushed by Claire rushing into my arms.

"Jimmy, Jimmy, Jimmy, you're back!" She shouted in that sultry voice. "I've missed you so much!" She shifted into that haunting nay-bray as she rocked her neck back and forth against my tight embrace, almost lifting me off my feet.

Everett stood back a respectful distance to allow us our moment. After we both had calmed, Claire gazed over my shoulder at the bowl.

"Eddie's garlic casserole, sweet!" As Claire dug into her meal, Everett met my gaze and shared,

We need to talk!

CHAPTER THIRTY-ONE
(Infamous iPhoney)

We'll be right back, Everett shared with Claire. He touched me on the shoulder, and we transported to his mancave.

No worries, Claire responded as we left, *I'll be out back working off this meal.*

Everett's ninety-inch flat screen was subdivided into twelve sections showing various viewpoints of Stella's Pink Pony Girl videos. As he started to digitally download the information, I stopped him.

No, let's do this slowly, in English, I don't want to miss anything.

He nodded, directed me to one of his extremely comfortable recliners, taking the other one, and began.

As you can see, there's been millions of views on each of these twelve videos. I've spent the time you were away tracking the IP addresses on every viewer. Once located, I then ran down their backgrounds. Most are the usual internet denizens and conspiracy theorists who could also be found trolling all of the paranormal websites and on-line forums, although some of them do not realize just how right they are when it comes to extra-terrestrials.

Anyway, some of the more technically savvy trolls hid their IP addresses using commercial grade companies like Tunnelbear, Cyber Ghost, SurfShark and Express VPN, which would stop any human technology or talented geek from peeking behind your security wall, maybe even some of the government security agencies, but it couldn't stop Michelle. Some creatively ran their footprints through Tor, but again, Michelle traced them. These geeks were all wetting themselves in excitement over these videos and calling for various local and televised paranormal groups to investigate the matter. But in the end, over time, they were ultimately distracted by the next interesting video or dropped off-line to take an extended pizza break.

Then there were a couple of troll trails that bounced around through proxy servers around the world but ultimately led to U.S. and foreign military and security service IP addresses. Again, it proved no match for Michelle's hacking skills. In the end, their techies and analysts were not any better than grandma's basement geeks, and basically regurgitated the speculation of their amateur counterparts. And the Intelligence Agencies were more caught up with spying on their own citizens during the 2020 election cycle, so they soon lost interest.

But there was one blind IP address that viewed each one of these videos, and after tracing it around the world several times to a server owned by the Grimm Twins' company, Gemini-2.N, Michelle ran into a brick wall. She had never seen security or encryption like this before, far superior to the technology employed by any human government.

Everett paused for a moment, transported to his bar, and returned with two tumblers of Macallan 12, Sherry Oak, without spilling a drop. Given that sherry was the alcohol of choice for the fairy godmothers, I had not tasted single malt in a long time. I closed my eyes and savored its rich aroma of dried fruits and wood spice, and then enjoyed its creamy flavor.

So, Michelle pulled out the big guns and brought Jayney in to help. Jayney got past the GN2 server security walls and traced the IP further to a blind VPN in Baker Oregon. There, Jayney ran into the Cas-Lux Artificial Intelligence system, which intercepted and then blocked Jayney from searching those final servers. Really impressive technology.

Everett took a long slow sip from his tumbler before continuing.

But not before Jayney had located the storage server containing all of the Pink Pony Girl videos up on the screen, plus this one.

Everett motioned to the flat screen and the twelve videos were replaced by one showing an iPhone video taken from one of the last of the cars sitting in cue on the day of the Pink Pony Girl event. The video shows the Longmont Fire Department Truck, sirens blasting, as it raced past the videographer's car in the oncoming lane and disappeared over the ridge down towards the cattle-jam below. The video then lowered from the driver's side window for a second for an unintentional shot of the owner's Ford Escape interior, and a really nice set of legs, while it recorded its young female driver's voice narrating her confusion and frustration over the traffic jam and her expressed worry about being late for a hair appointment. Then it rose back to window level and recorded our Toyota just as it came alongside her vehicle in the oncoming lane. You can see the silhouettes of the figures in our car well enough to get a head count, but it was not really clear enough to identify the occupants. The video continued to follow the Toyota until it has almost completely passed the sitting Ford. Just before you could make out the Toyota's rear license plate, the SUV and occupant dematerialized, to the soundtrack of the videographer's sing-song string of creative expletives to memorialize her astonishment.

Fuck me! Was all I could come up with. Everett refilled my tumbler before I realized it had left my hand.

The Cas-Lux AI system -

- Is owned by the Twin Brothers Grimm. I finished his thought.

"And the Baker Oregon IP address disappeared from the Internet that very night." Everett shifted to aural communication.

"Any strangers snooping around the area since then?" I asked.

"Not a peep since those two metrosexuals were sniffing around Grandpa's Café and Side Tracked back in March of last year."

"Thank God for small miracles." I whispered before emptying the last of the tumbler.

But God must have gotten busy with other matters after that.

CHAPTER THIRTY-TWO
(Getting Settled)

The children chased the Sprites out back along the edge of the pond on the strictest of orders that, while they were allowed to run fast, they had to move like humans. No teleporting.

Claire happily stepped right into the role of 'Outside Nanny.' She kept close watch on the children as they ran and shrieked and shouted while the Sprites, looking no more than like dragon flies to any human observer from a distance, avoided the children's reach with aerial acrobatics that would defy human physics. It would also explain how they evaded my local bat population. The kids looked like cats chasing moving laser dots on a wall. We could sense Claire's sultry admonishments whenever they came too close to crossing any Tellurian-Centaurian movement lines or to actually falling into the pond itself. When they were sufficiently exhausted they would all sit around by the edge of the pond with the children pointing at various forms of the wildlife while Claire instructed them on each creature's role in the natural order of things and explained some of their more unique traits. Claire was one umbrella short of being their outdoor Mary Poppins. If she could sing, she would have given Maria von Trapp a run for her money as well.

Gina and I spent our free time getting caught up on our daily lives. I checked on all of the investments, updated my automatic trading schedules and made sure that there were the occasional losses to some of the accounts to keep any government oversight agencies from taking a second look at them. Over the past year, the accountant that Helen had hooked me up with when we arrived, Robert Kunisch, in nearby Loveland, had kept me on the financial straight and narrow. He had access to my domestic accounts and made sure all of the reportable quarterly tax filings and payments went into the appropriate agencies on time. I also reached out to the Gibraltar firms that were handling my overseas trusts to make sure there were no hick-ups that would bring undue attention to them. In the end, everything was quiet on the money front, and I remained a wealthy intergalactic hybrid.

I had no way of knowing at that time that my on-line transactions were being monitored beyond the governmental regulatory gatekeepers that I anticipated and planned for. By the time I learned the truth, it was too late.

Gina spent the day preparing the meal and making me prepare the house for the arrival of the rest of the crew. Eddie had done such a bang-up job at keeping our home in meticulous condition, that I really only had to make sure the outdoor table was in good shape and wiped down, that there were enough chairs for the anticipated guests and that we had sufficient refreshments and snacks to appeal to everyone's palates. A quick trip in my new Ford 150 XLT to Hometown Liquors and Hays Market in Berthoud took care of most of it. Easy peasy.

Lenny was the first to arrive in his black SUV and was almost knocked clear of the driver's seat as an overly excited Blue came flying past him and leapt into the waiting arms of Gina, where the large black Pitbull exuberantly licked her happy pet-parent's face. If Gina was still in her old human form, that dog's aerial arrival would have done some serious damage.

Maeve patiently followed Lenny out of the SUV as the tall and lanky U.S. Marshall gave me a welcoming embrace.

"I'd ask if you are just really happy to see me," I teased, "but I know that's just your 45."

"Leave comedy to us humans, Jimmy," Lenny retorted, laughing, and patting his concealed handgun before he forcefully jettisoned me for the now freed up Gina, Blue having led Maeve over the side fence and down towards the backyard.

"You guys are going to have to fix me up with one of your Centaurian sisters," Lenny said as he gave Gina a kiss on the cheek and an affectionate squeeze. "I'll admit that Jimmy's Centauri transition was a definite upgrade, I mean, God, he couldn't get any uglier, but you my dear are just as pretty as ever."

"Don't I know it," Gina said with as much New York sass as she could muster, then winked at me, "and don't you forget it."

I thought I sensed the name *Petrichor* flash quickly through her mind.

"Did I hear someone was looking to date a perfect Centaurian female?" Michelle said as she materialized on our front porch and stepped down into the driveway. Everett appeared and went right into his spiel with "Who said Centaurians were not funny? A human, a werewolf and a mule walked into a bar. . ."

"Who does a guy have to shoot to get a drink around here?" Lenny cackled, hugging Michelle and Everett simultaneously with both arms.

"Shoot Jimmy," Everett deadpanned over Lenny's shoulder, "it doesn't stick with him."

"Did I hear someone mention 'werewolf?'" Whitey howled as he came walking into view from around the end in the road, leapt the front fence upright without touching it and raced across the front property, almost tackling me when he reached the group.

"Or mule?" Claire said as she arrived at the top of her side paddock.

"Holy shit!" Lenny bellowed as he saw the size of Stella and Apollo, both standing next to Claire.

"Do you kiss your mother with that mouth?" Claire challenged playfully, "There's children present."

"Not since I buried her." Lenny responded as he leaned across the fence and gave Claire a gentle chuck under the chin, and then turned to the children. "Come over here and give your Uncle Lenny a hug!"

I downloaded my full memory of Lenny and nodded to the children.

Take Uncle Lenny down to the backyard. I instructed.

Can we transport him? Apollo asked.

Just as fast as you can. I responded.

The two kids teleported over the fence to Lenny, with Apollo hugging him tightly around his neck and Stella around his waist. Then, before Lenny could catch his breath, all three disappeared.

"Why you little bastards!" Lenny shouted from the back yard.

The two children reappeared, laughing hysterically. Claire joined in with her Lurchy laugh.

"C'mon," Gina said to the group, "Let's shift this to the back dining area. The others should be arriving shortly."

Michelle reached out her hands to the kids and all three disappeared.

You all go ahead. I shared with the others. *I'll wait for the rest and be down shortly.*

I'll wait up here with you, Jimmy. Claire responded.

Won't be long, Bobbi piped in. *We stopped to pick up Eileen and we're right around the corner. The girls just picked up Lucian and will be there in a moment.*

True to her word, a large black Econoline with the logo The Oracle artfully emblazoned on its side panel in gold leaf, turned off of Beverly Drive and onto our driveway from the east, followed moments later by Scarlett and Savanna's black Sahara Jeep from the west.

Helen exited the driver's side of the van and hurried around to help Bobbi out of the passenger's side while Eileen appeared out of the side sliding door carrying some unidentifiable bottles in both hands.

The two young ladies leapt from the jeep and raced past The Oracle crew to excitedly embrace an ecstatic Claire, before making their rounds to the other adults, while Lucian, now a half foot taller than a year before, embraced Whitey first, then followed the girls through the gauntlet of the engaging crowd. Eddie avoided everyone entirely as he carried a large fragrant wicker basket filled with Greek pastries directly through the side gate.

"Who does a guy got to shoot to get a meal around here." Bellowed Lenny from the back yard.

"I don't think he's kidding." Bobbi giggled.

"I'll see you all out back," Gina said, "I have to check on dinner."

"I'll give you a hand," Helen chimed in.

Good to be home, isn't it Jimmy? Bobbi shared.

I watched as the rest of the group, already engaging in catch-up conversations, filed through the side gate, and headed down towards the back of the house.

Sure is, I responded. As I closed the side gate behind me, I waited as the others proceeded down the hill and around the corner. I looked out towards the front edge of my property and thought about how important this house, its occupants and visitors had become to me. But in that moment I could not shake the feeling of apprehension that was just sitting there, tucked away in the back of my mind. I turned and walked down the path alone, wondering how long I would be able to protect this growing family of mine and at what lengths would I go to keep them all safe.

CHAPTER THIRTY-THREE
(The New Normal)

Eddie and Helen had just cleared the table of the dessert dishes, and coffee cups were replaced by crystal tumblers and shot glasses. Gina excused herself in order to put the children to bed, and after performing a hug circuit at Centaurian speed, Apollo and Stella bid everyone good night and disappeared with Gina. Scarlett, Savanna and Lucian bid their farewells and promised to return the next day after their classes.

"Are we still on for that shooting lesson?" Lucian asked Whitey.

"I'll bring the rifles." Whitey responded. "Can we use your Boulder range, Lenny?"

"Sure," Lenny responded. "But maybe you want an expert to show you instead, eh, Loosh?"

"This boy's a natural," Whitey said. "But maybe you should tag along, so I can show him what not to do."

That brought the usual razzing as the youngsters slipped out of the backyard, waving as they exited.

"Put that Scottish swill away and taste this Irish classic!" Eileen shouted over the buzzing of the remaining adult members of the group around the dinner table. She then distributed generous portions of clear liquid from her unlabeled glass bottles she had stowed by the foot of her chair.

"Potcheen! Irish moonshine," she cackled, devilishly. "This will put hair on your chest."

Lenny was the first brave soul to down his shot as soon as the topped off glass reached him. "Whoa," he gasped, shaking the demons from his head, "that's got the kick of a mule! No offense, Claire."

"None taken," Claire responded, breaking into her deep throated laughter.

"Potato whiskey. One hundred-eighty proof, the secret is in the quadruple distillation. I grow my own peat for the fire." Eileen bragged. "Family recipe."

Whitey lifted his shot glass and stood. "To our misfits!"

Everyone else stood and waited while Lenny quickly refilled his shot glass.

"Slainte!" Lenny signaled and we all tossed back our shots.

I waited for the expected burning sensation to my trachea and was pleasantly surprised when none arrived. This liquor was smooth to the palate but its immediate impact on your body was palpable. Your chest was instantly warmed, and your heart started to pound, causing a deep and sharp intake of breath. I could feel Spaghetti dancing a jig in the back of my mind. No wonder the Irish loved to fight; this stuff put beer muscles to shame.

The two Centaurians slammed their shot glasses down simultaneously, and with eyes closed, they found each other's hands for a solid high five. "That's what I'm talking about," whispered Michelle.

Whitey let out a howl that was surely going to be mentioned in tomorrow's Nextdoor postings.

"Jesus, Whitey!" Gina admonished as she materialized in the spot beside me. "I just got the kids off to sleep."

"Sorry, Gina, that slipped out," Whitey apologized, while the rest of the crowd quieted in complicity.

"Well, come on now," Gina said, grabbing an empty shot glass and tapping it on the table. "Let's find out what all the fuss is about!"

Eileen obliged with a wink and a pour, and Gina threw her shot back like a New York construction worker on payday.

"Oh, that's special." She gasped, appreciatively staring at the empty shot glass.

Another round was poured, but before it could be consumed, Bobbi stood, raised her hands to calm the masses and, having gotten their undivided attention, addressed the crew.

"It seems that we spend a lot of time welcoming Jimmy back here to his own home," Bobbi began.

"Any excuse for a party!" Lenny interjected.

"But we must not forget that it was Jimmy that brought us all together in the first place," Bobbi continued, ignoring the peanut gallery, "he opened his home to us."

"Our home is your home," Gina responded affectionately, the Potcheen having its desired effect.

"Thank you, Gina," Bobbi said respectfully, before continuing. "And since this is now 'our home,' we need to do everything in our collective power to protect it." She stood there silently thinking about what she would say next, blocking any and all who tried to peek behind the curtain.

"The world is going to shit around us," Bobbi said. "A plague has been unleashed from across the oceans on the human populace, killing the old, the weak, and the infirm. And this new United States government has used this disease as an excuse to cross the portals of every household, uninvited. I fear what will happen if they ever cross this threshold."

"I know what will happen to the first thirty," Whitey shouted. "They can have my long gun only after I empty it. And after that the unlucky ones get the wolf."

"But that's not the primary threat Spirit has been warning me about," Bobbi said, "there is something more insidious, and I can't get a clearer picture other than when they do come, they will come first for the most powerful of us all. So, from this moment on, we must all be extra vigilant of everything around us and watch out for one another."

Bobbi lifted her shot glass and stared at the rest of us. We all raised our glasses in response.

"To end my warning with a quote from the Bard, who stole it from my sisterhood," Bobbi somberly toasted, "Something wicked this way comes."

CHAPTER THIRTY-FOUR
(Bad Ass Women)

Everett stood up after Bobbi and took everyone through what his investigation over the past year had uncovered about the Grimm Twins, Victor and Seth Beauseigneur, their company G2N and the Cas-Lux AI system.

"I've always considered the tech oligarchs on this planet as a necessary evil to humankind's advancement to full space exploration. Their innate selfishness and narcissism are what drives them to develop the technological innovations you will need to truly break free of this planet." Everett began. "But these twin mirrored assholes have taken it up to a whole different level. From everything I could discover using my most advanced detection methods, they have convinced themselves that they are preternatural, and given their respective and conjoined IQs, they are probably right. But where the other tech oligarchs have been willing to share even their most innovative discoveries for the right price, these two are sharing only a watered-down version of their cutting-edge AI system with the government. They are keeping their alpha program for themselves."

"Who gives a shit about these twin fuckers and their Asshole Intelligence!" Lenny shouted, definitely embracing the effects of the potcheen.

"We all will, soon enough," Everett responded with more force than expected. "They have been the ones showing the most interest in the internet buzz on the Pink Pony Girl, even after all of this time. They have reached out and bought up every video taken that day and their AI has expunged any mention of the Pink Pony Girl or her videos from the internet."

"That explains it," Bobbi confirmed. "Spirit has warned me that no single human would dare to challenge us. There will be two faces, like the god Janus, and it will hold the key to the door to the future."

"Well, I will match this god Anus's keys, doors and faces with my bullets," Lenny responded. "Nobody that draws a breath for existence will harm this family and live to brag about it."

"Damn right!" Eddie seconded.

"I won't charge any extra to rip both faces off them," Whitey added.

"Let's turn down the testosterone, gentlemen," Eileen shouted. "Everett has the floor!"

"I'm warning you all, these two present the clearest danger to this family." Everett said.

"Let's hear the rest," I said.

Everett explained in detail how the brothers' AI system had thwarted Jayney's attempt to fully drill down on the Grimm Twins and how all traces of their IP address had immediately disappeared from the internet. Finally, Everett explained how the Grimm Twins were also in possession of a video of our Toyota when Apollo did his David Copperfield impersonation and dematerialized the Rav 4.

"I dumped the Toyota," Whitey interrupted. "Sank like a stone in the deepest part of Crater lake. There were no witnesses. I ran home taking the scenic route through the woods and over open fields, just to make sure I didn't pass any vehicles on the way out."

"And I hacked and sanitized the DMV servers of any reference to the existence of that car or its relationship to Jimmy Moran," Michelle added.

"I'd still love to know if anyone comes looking for that information," Lenny said, sobered by the news he was absorbing, "but I don't want to raise any suspicions asking the powers that be on my end to set up any techy-traps, now that you've scrubbed the file."

"I can set up a honeypot, so anyone outside the DMV who attempts to hack the DMV servers for that specific information would be rerouted to a dead end, but we'd have their IP fingerprints and could trace it back to the source." Michelle explained.

"Sounds like a plan," Lenny said. "Although I don't need to know the details, I have a hard enough time programming my TV remote."

"What did your Spirit guide mean by 'they will come first for the most powerful of us all?'" Gina pivoted the conversation back towards Bobbi.

"And, from a human perspective, who would that be?" Eileen added.

"Can't say for sure," Bobbi answered. "How do you measure that? We are all so different."

"I've witnessed all of us in action," I volunteered, "and right now, if I were to make that call, it would be Michelle."

"Pity the fool!" Lenny added.

"Ain't that the truth." Claire seconded.

"Let them come then," Michelle said resolutely.

"But we are not sure what we're up against here." Everett interjected, worriedly. "I mean, this isn't the mafia, and look at the damage *they* did before we ended it. The AI Jayney ran into was pretty damn sophisticated for any human to have created. Who knows what those twins have in their quiver?"

"But unlike our battle with the mafia," Michelle responded, "this time, I'm not going to be limited to observer status. Centauri rules be damned. They come for me, or any one of us, I will terminate their existence, and that of anyone that comes with them."

"Everett," Lenny said, grabbing the potcheen bottle out of Eileen's hand and taking a long swig from it, "with all due respect, your lady is hot!"

Eileen snatched the bottle back from him and drew a long pull from it as well. "Amen to that!"

"Can't argue there!" Eddie added.

Whitey let out a low short howl.

"And you call us animals?" Claire responded indignantly, before laughing. "Who am I kidding, that was kinda hot."

"Don't I know it," Everett said as Michelle leaned over and gave him a kiss.

"I got Greek warrior blood coursing through my veins, Eddie and Lenny know fifty ways to kill someone without getting dirty and Bobbi, as soft as she is, has permanent wi-fi and mother nature in her hip pocket, so we are in," Helen weighed in, "but what about the youngsters?"

"They're all pretty good with handguns," Lenny stated.

"And long guns," Whitey added, "especially Lucian."

"Too risky," I interjected. "They are just going to have to stay clear until we get a better handle on what's coming down the pike."

"And what about Apollo and Stella?" Bobbi asked.

"Anyone comes near my kids," Gina answered, channeling what was left of her deep Italian roots, "They'll wish Michelle got to them first."

"You go, sister!" Michelle responded proudly. "The Amazons got nothing on the Centauri."

Whitey let out another low howl.

With that, Lenny started tapping his empty shot glass on the table, rapidly joined by the others. This time, I poured the entire round of Potcheen at Centauri speed, and was back at my chair beside Gina before the last tap subsided without spilling a drop.

I stood there, met each of their gazes, and offered a toast, "to all bad ass women, and the men. . . and women . . . who love them!"

CHAPTER THIRTY-FIVE
(Olympus Threatens)

When you are dealing with mafia reprisals, there are rules of engagement that have been formed since before the time of the Romans. They also have a code of honor that they uphold and rigorously enforce amongst their own. They are relentless and will come for you. But there are things that they just will not do, like hurt a child of tender years. That allows you to plan and strategize and meet them on the field of battle. Do not get me wrong, they are brutal and ruthless, but win or lose, the game is fair. So, truth be told, under their rules, I had it coming the night of the Storm two years ago when Dan Pearsall put that bullet through my heart, and Dan was equally deserving of the responding 9mm magazine that Gina emptied into him. It is humanity at its most base. But rules are rules.

The Grimm Twins were a new breed of enemy. Their mirrored genius created a heightened level of narcissism that allowed them to believe that no rules applied to them. The groundwork for this kind of thinking had been laid over the recent years by the other alphabet tech oligarchies. Northern California was the new Olympus, and they were its new gods. They had taken over the world and they could do whatever they wanted. You defied them at your peril. They controlled the lightening.

The first to realize this were slick governmental operatives and the media, who could never generate power on their own but fed like parasites off of the power of others. The operatives watched carefully as the supremacy of the older, titans of industry – steel, automotive, railway, consumer goods, and unions – waned and they were ready to worship at the altar of their more powerful offspring – information – when during the Titanomachy of the twenty-first century, it overthrew its parents. Since all gods need to be worshipped, the impotent modern priesthood of government and media were ready to foster and proselytize the new religion and reap their reward from the gods. They, in turn, got to impose their will on the masses and if you objected, you got the lightening from their benefactors.

But what these technological upstarts and their sycophants did not understand was that they did not invent lightening. Nor did the titans before them. They should have studied their classics, especially the Theogony of Hesiod, because they were about to experience the Chaos from which all things arose.

But until the Grimm Twin gods came down from Olympus to Berthoud looking for a fight, we were happy to ignore them. And that is what we did, but we slept with one eye open.

CHAPTER THIRTY-SIX
(Passing the Parcel)

The new me that was born the night of the Storm had a lot of cool superpowers the old me could only dream of. But I still maintained most of the emotional and psychological limitations that lead to a lot of bad decisions I made when I was totally human. And while I was happy to share my positive attributes with my children, I sure as hell did not want to burden them with the negatives. So, I made sure that they both filled up on not only my and Gina's good things, but the best that each of the other members of the crew had to offer. The better things you place in your basket, the less room is left for the bad things. Fill your shopping cart with fruits and veggies and you will have no place to put the ice cream.

And the crew stepped up big time. You see, they each realized that Stella and Apollo presented a *tabula rasa*, and Gina and I had just handed them our painter's pallet. They had each already shared their respective gifts in a more limited, passive fashion on the substantially formed Scarlett, Savanna and Lucian, but now they could pull out all of the stops when it came to our two hybrids. After all, the older children were only human. The crew also realized that these two children were the only paintings they as a family were going to be leaving behind, so they better be *objet d'art*.

Bobbi stepped into Bonnie's role and continued teaching Stella how to mix her advanced genetic abilities with old-world magic. They would sit together crossed-legged by the pond for hours in perfect meditative silence, their minds interlocked but blocked from the predation of all others, until some unexpected manifestation of nature, like a powerful dust devil on a windless day or a nearby lightning strike from a clear sky, caused them both to leap to their feet and, locking hands, dance in celebratory circles.

And while Apollo was anointed the protector of the ABC Sprites by Bonnie, it was very clear that under Bobbi's tutelage, they attended Stella like ladies in waiting.

Bobbi also figured out, with the assistance of her dead Strega grandmother, that Stella's Fairy King's Diamond in her necklace could be used like the end of a wand to direct energy from her mind through the stone to another object, almost like a laser. After a while, Stella was able to focus the energy beam with enough power to disintegrate the various sized quartz stones that littered our back property. The quartz would absorb the beam until it reached critical load and then vaporize.

Michelle became both children's resource for all things Centaurian. And Gina sat in for all of these sessions, treating them like her own continuing ed classes. I never fully appreciated human history beyond the myths and fables, and I sure did not care about what happened on another planet before mankind walked upright, but Gina, Stella and Apollo accepted download after download with the same excitement I showed watching Marx Brothers movies. I was all for making history, just not interested in remembering it. If I ever needed an answer to the question of who ruled Centauri ten thousand years ago, I knew who to ask.

Lenny, Whitey and Eddie were upset that Gina would not let them teach Stella and Apollo human weaponry until they were a little older – I stayed out of it – so they limited themselves to sharing what they each had observed of the human condition through their respective viewpoints.

Lenny shared stories of his life as a U.S. Marshall. He did not focus so much on the concept of enforcing laws, especially given that he was prone to break them when it suited his needs, but he did emphasize through his stories that the truly good person always protects the innocent.

Eddie taught the children the meaning of camaraderie, of working together with others as a group, especially when attacked by outsiders. He reinforced the concept that no matter what, you never left anyone behind.

Whitey taught the children everything there was to know about the feral natural world, and that the same concepts of protecting the innocent, loyalty to your group, and the need to be willing to defend both to the death, transgressed all species. He also shared his family's Nordic myths and legends, and it was during those lessons that I audited his classes.

Everett and I would take the children out during the witching hour for flights in Jayney. Stella was thrilled that the ship's AI sounded like her mother, although the first time she heard that voice I could see the memories of her times with Petrichor flashing through her mind, before she realized I was peeking, and shut me out. Despite the fact that both kids had grown to the size of second graders, it was still unbelievable to see them each taking turns controlling this ship. They took to it with the confidence of youth, having been never told in their short lives that there was something they could not do. Surprisingly, Apollo was more of a natural at the controls than Stella. He must have gotten Gina's genes.

Helen taught the children the basic principle of business success, which was that if they wanted something bad enough, they had to go after it. They could not wait for someone else to give it to them. She shared with them every memory she·had from the time when she was a little girl, where she was told she could not have or do something because of who she was. They loved the stories she shared about her Uncle Gus, and I was thrilled to see that they could laugh at his antics with the abandon of human children.

The biggest surprise was Eileen, who, given her own expertise in both human and animal biology, readily stepped into the role vacated by Tessa, and taught the children all the more advanced math and sciences right through university level. But like Tessa, Eileen demanded that they learn it the old-fashioned way, like humans.

These educational rotations not only kept the children always in the presence of one of the adults but also kept the adults consistently rolling through the homestead. And that way I could keep an eye on everyone.

The totally human branch of our family of misfits, Scarlett, Savanna and Lucian, accepted their banishment as a matter of trust. Michelle and Gina had sat them down and explained that there was an unknown danger lurking in the shadows and that this was the only way to protect them. I missed their presence at the homestead. Their total humanity had kept me grounded. But that same feature made me worry for them. I set up extensive trust funds for each of them just in case things went south on our end. Hope for the best but plan for the worst.

And with Bobbi's warning ever in my mind, I became Michelle's nightmare by constantly reaching out to check on her at all hours of the day and night, to the point where she finally and literally told me to "fuck off" – that she is perfectly capable of protecting herself, and that, in the unfathomable chance that she ever needed my "hybrid help," she would let me know. Then she totally blocked me. Undeterred, I thereafter pestered Everett to keep me posted on Michelle's comings and goings.

That is how our family of misfits continued through to the end of the summer of 2021. The world outside our compound fought back to a semblance of the new normal through the mass administration to the fearful and vulnerable of the miracle vaccine program developed by the party no longer in power, while the healthy humans refused the shot and continued to combat the virus the way mother nature had intended, through suffering the virus' effects and developing natural antibodies until herd immunity had been reached. That did not satisfy the new government, and there were whispers of coming mandates and a resulting class system that would torment the resistance.

Stores slowly started to reopen, and the quaking sheep started to lose their facemasks when driving alone in their vehicles or running alone through mountain trails. Nonetheless, the new government, often through edicts issued from the altars of their media priests by their titular medical gnome, would occasionally reinstate their draconian lockdown measures just to make sure they still could impose their will on the misinformed and the broken. With the common will sufficiently crushed under the pretense of the virus, the government slowly introduced additional measures having nothing to do with COVID to ensure that its citizens would be unable to oppose it ever again. It was hard to believe I was ever a part of this world and could not help but root for mafia families I had left back east – who I knew would never bow their heads. I had concluded that the human race deserved to have its candy taken from them.

And that is how the world looked the weekend of the now lifeless Labor Day Holiday of 2021, when a black Sikorsky S-92 dropped silently from the clouds and landed on the soccer field area in the back of my property.

CHAPTER THIRTY-SEVEN
(Twin Peaks Comes To Mohammed)

Despite the extrasensory smorgasbord surrounding the backyard table that Saturday afternoon, enjoying the last of the barbeque spread Helen had provided, it was Claire's natural mule hearing that first picked up on the otherwise silent aircraft.

Incoming. She shared with the rest as she lifted her head from her bowl of veggies and turned towards the back property. We all stopped what we were doing and followed her gaze.

Claire was not happy. She considered everything beyond the immediate backyard area behind the house to be her fiefdom. Family could come and go, but strangers were not welcome.

This helicopter that dropped from the clouds was so dark, the surrounding sunshine seemed to be sucked into it like a black hole. I could barely make out the row of five windows on the side, or the larger glass opening on the door towards the rear of the craft. It was virtually silent as it made a final rotation and then settled softly onto the open space, kicking up the red Colorado dust into the air around it. The alarmed red wing black birds rose in unison from the billowing grass surrounding the adjoining pond and headed out over the property to the west.

Michelle, could you take the kids over to your place? I requested.

You may need me here. She replied, maneuvering her body in human fashion to the side of the table closest to the back property.

We need you to protect Apollo and Stella. Gina shared. *No matter what.*

Michelle and Everett traded glances but not thoughts.

Michelle reached over and took the children's hands in her own and walked them through the sliding back doors and into the interior shadows before disappearing.

Whitey was holding the now growling Maeve and Blue by their collars, but I could see the hair on the back of Whitey's neck rising like the hackles on the two large dogs.

I'll lock them up in the house, he shared, then led them, resisting, inside. *I'll be up in the tower window with the AR in case you need me. The pilot gets it first.*

Lenahan reached into his belt, removed his Glock 45 from its holster, released the safety and then chambered a round. He did the same for the second weapon, a Sig P365 he removed from his ankle holster, and then slid it across the table to Eddie, who tucked in into his belt and then moved to the seat at the farthest end of the table. Lenny left his weapon in plain sight on the table before him.

"Stay calm everyone," Bobbi said softly, "Spirit says that it's all going to be fine."

"That's all fine and good," Lenny responded, his eyes focused on the chopper, "but tell Spirit that if he gets it wrong and I end up on the wrong side of the veil today, I'm going to whip his ass."

The chopper blades slowed their rotation and we all watched as the side door to the craft opened.

Fuck me, it's those Grimm Twins. Everett shared, his scanning technique still a step ahead of my own.

A bunch of suits climbed out of the helicopter. Three of them looked to be in their thirties, wore nicer clothing than I ever sported as a lawyer, and took defensive positions around the perimeter of the craft, opening the buttons on their jackets as they did so. Each had an automatic weapon slung over their shoulder.

"You see that, Eddie?" Lenny called over without taking his eyes off them. "All packing."

"Got 'em." Eddie replied.

The pilot, who looked to be in his forties, wearing khakis, a flight jacket, and aviator sunnies that made him look like the POTUS, then exited his door and quickly marched around the opposite side of the craft, where he met two tall and thin twenty-somethings exiting the chopper. They were wearing matching Southampton summer chic outfits, that would have looked right at home in the stands at the U.S. Open. The pilot pointed in our direction and then fell in behind the twins as they made their way across the back field in our direction. The thirty-somethings in suits carved their own paths through the high grass to stay on a perimeter of the twins.

Everett scanned their minds and provided an aural report to Lenny and Eddie as they approached.

"The young man on the left with the shoulder length Jheri curls is Joseph Serrano. They call him 'Carl.' Did a few tours in the middle east with Uncle Sam and then a stint with Blackwater before joining the Twins' security team.

"The man on the far right with the seventies moustache is Michael 'Disco' Augustyni, another grunt who spent most of his time during his middle east tours circulating among forward operating bases in Iraq before the pull out. He worked with G4S for a half dozen years before signing on with the Twins.

"The tall one in the rear is Brian Cory. He goes by his anagram, 'B.C.' He worked as a field agent throughout the 'Stans' bordering Russia for the CIA before being recruited to head up the Twins travelling security team.

"The pilot is Joe Dzikas, a retired Lieutenant Colonel in the U.S. Airforce, handles the overall security for the Twins, including their Baker Oregon ranch, and is qualified to fly pretty much anything. He is the only one the twins will fly with. Everyone calls him 'Colonel.'"

"That just leaves Tweedle Dee and Tweedle Dum," Lenny responded.

Claire ambled nonchalantly over to the fence line by the back gate just as the Twins and their entourage arrived at the other side of it. Then she dumped a massive shit in their path and waited while they had to leap over its steaming pile to enter the backyard before slipping through the still open gate behind them and trotting down towards the parked chopper.

I'll be down here if you need me. Claire shared.

The twins were as identical as any pair I had ever seen. They looked like a couple of teens, with matching thick hairlines and their brown manes cropped short and imperfect, as if they cut it themselves. Their skin was pink and flawless, and they shared matching sets of emerald, green eyes. Both wore wispy goatees, the kind you would expect to see sprouting from the chin of a virile fourteen-year-old.

Neither twin spoke to the other men or each other as they approached. Their minds were completely still, like they were in deep meditation. I could only draw the image of a flame in either of their minds.

The security detail fanned out and when the one with the Jheri curls started to circle up hill and around the side of the house, Lenny called him out.

"That's far enough, sonny" Lenny said, displaying his shield and resting his hand on his 45.

I did not need to read Serrano's mind to see that he was making his own calculations as to whether he could draw down on Lenny. I could sense Eddie's full attention on Disco, who seemed to be distracted on scanning the upper windows of the house.

I got this douchebag, Whitey shared from the Tower.

"This is Seth and Victor Beauseigneur," Joe Dzikas said, breaking the ice with as light a tone as he could muster.

"Welcome," Gina said, standing up and approaching the duo. BC moved in an intercepting fashion from behind the brothers. The twin on the left raised his right hand to stop him, and then continued his movement forward as he extended that hand towards Gina. She grasped and gave it a solid shake in a manner that would make my dear dead father proud. I could see the wince in the lead Twin's eyes as she released her grip.

"Seth Beauseigneur," the left twin offered. His voice was surprisingly deep.

"Gina Moran," Gina responded.

"And this is his brother, Victor," Dzikas continued. Gina repeated her introduction with repeated effect, but the other twin did not say anything.

I noticed Seth's eyes scrutinizing the tableware, far too much for our present number.

"I'm sorry," Seth said, "have we interrupted a party?"

Spirit says to watch these bastards. Bobbi shared.

They look like a couple of stoners. Claire interjected.

"Couple of last-minute cancellations," I covered. "Positive COVID tests."

Helen stood up and started clearing the plates, then carried the platter in through the back door.

And that is when I heard their strange language. It was telepathic. It reminded me of when I first heard Spaghetti speaking Irish with Junkie.

It's their own language. Common among twins. Each unique. Everett shared. *I can't decipher it.*

Seth turned to his brother, and I spotted what looked like a brown cochlear implant on the rear side of Seth's skull, nestled in his thick hairline. I scrutinized Victor's hairline and located his matching version on the mirror side.

That's the telepathic receiver the brothers had implanted. Everett observed.

Victor shared the image of the Pink Pony Girl and the Toyota. But there was something else, some other presence lurking in the background of the brothers' telepathic exchanges. A fleeting sentient shadow.

"So, to what do we owe this honor?" I asked. "I don't remember inviting the Grimm twins and your friends to my party."

The telepathic chatter increased between the two brothers, and I could see that Victor was getting anxious. Dealing with people was really painful for him.

"May I speak frankly, Mr. Moran?" Seth said. He was clearly the dominant twin.

"I wish you would," I responded, with just a hint of impatience.

"A little over a year ago," Seth continued, "an event occurred in this general area, that involved a special little girl."

Joe Dzikas removed an iPad from the shoulder bag he was carrying and opened it up to the Pink Pony Girl videos he had collected from you tube.

I feigned interest in watching the videos, and then closed the screen.

"Yeah, I remember hearing about that. She's a cutey." I said, offering the Colonel his iPad back. "So, what does this have to do with me?"

Seth was watching my performance with almost disdain. Victor was obviously getting more impatient by the second. The telepathic chatter increased, and I saw the image of the Toyota flash between them.

"Show him," Seth ordered the Colonel.

His minion opened the iPad screen and this time he showed me the video of Toyota and its disappearing act.

"We believe the little girl in question may have left the scene in this SUV," the Colonel said. "Your SUV."

"Wow, that was quite an exit." I responded, adding a whistle for emphasis. "But I don't own a Toyota."

This time it was the Colonel that seemed to be getting impatient, so I took a moment to peek into his brain, and that is when I saw it. I was not sure how he got his hands on it, but there was an image of a schedule from my last year's federal income tax form, showing the deductions my accountant had taken for the annual Colorado state taxes I paid, including the annual registration fees I paid on my Toyota. Had to give it to them for thinking outside the DMV box. I sure as hell missed it.

"Are your sure about that Mr. Moran?" the Colonel queried just a little to patronizingly. He started to reach back into his satchel.

"Colonel," Seth interrupted him. "I'm sure Mr. Moran knows what cars he owns."

I looked back into Seth's mind and there, behind the telepathic babel he was exchanging with Victor was that other presence. I could not get a fix on it.

"So, why are you so interested in finding this girl?" I asked him.

"Because she obviously has gifts beyond the present evolutionary level of mankind," Seth responded, "and my brother and I want to study her, learn from her."

Be her! Victor's mind let that bit of English slip.

"The Beauseigneurs are willing to invest their considerable resources in ensuring that this young lady has the best of everything." The Colonel added, like a car salesman trying to sell you on the importance of that special undercoating just before closing the deal. "She can live the life of a princess."

Now the Colonel had his iPad out again, showing us what looked like the interior of a palace, with everything a young human child could ever want.

"The Beausiegnuers have spared no expense to provide everything that this young girl could need." The Colonel continued, "And you would, of course, have scheduled visiting days each month at the brothers' compound in Oregon."

Get rid of these assholes or I will. Shared Gina.

Say the word, Jimmy. Whitey offered.

I'll nail any of the stragglers before they get back to the chopper! Claire voted.

We can find the Hadron Distributor and shrink that chopper, Everett added, *it is somewhere in that pond.*

Fuck it, Michelle chimed in from across the road, *I'll drop the whole thing into Crater lake myself, as is.*

I searched the minds of the security team and the Colonel to find one reason not to kill them all by my own hand, starting with the twins, but came up empty. In fact, the sociopathic darkness I found brewing in the minds of each of them supported my channeling my inner Valachi. *Protect the family.*

Let them go, Jimmy, Bobbi counseled. *Spirit says there are too many eyes watching these brothers. It won't end here.*

"I think it's time for you, Victor and your friends to go, Seth." I said.

"But Mr. Moran —" the Colonel countered.

"You heard the man." Lenny added, standing and taking his 45 into his hand. Eddie also rose to his feet and raised his shirt, exposing his weapon.

Carl and Disco suddenly became animated, their minds telegraphing that they were spoiling for a firefight. BC's eyes twitched, and were suddenly drawn upwards, and I could see his mind's vision of the sun glinting off a metallic movement in the Tower window. It visualized the concept of "sniper" on the first pass.

"Stand down," BC ordered the other two. "Colonel, we should escort the Beauseigneurs back to the chopper."

The Grim Twins exchanged their telepathic gibberish with that other presence shadowing their thoughts. And then, like a flash, I saw images of my entire previous life as Jimmy McCarthy downloading into the twins' minds. The conversion was not digital, but it was some form of code.

Cas-Lux! Everett shared. *The brothers are tapped into their AI.*

Fuck this! Gina lost it. Before I could stop her she had disarmed the entire security team and tossed their completely disassembled firearms onto the ground in a heap. You never saw her move. She just appeared before them, the anger flashing in her Nordic blue eyes.

"I'm not going to ask you again. Leave now!" She hissed at the twins. "Next time you come here it will be you in pieces."

The Colonel hurriedly ushered the Grim Twins back across the yard and out through the back gate towards their waiting chopper, and Victor shrieked as he stepped into the still steaming package Claire had left for them. The security team never took their eyes off us as they carefully followed up the rear.

That went well! Claire shared, as she stood off to the side of the soccer field and watched the chopper rise into the air.

"Holy crap!" Bobbi shouted. "Dan Pearsall just came through. He said, 'it's time to go to the mattresses, Jimmy.'"

CHAPTER THIRTY-EIGHT
(O Danny Boy)

I guess things really are different in Heaven. While I only got one good foot in that door the night I died, I have been told by reputable sources that before you cross the threshold of the pearly gates you must leave all of humanity's pettiness on the doorstep. Indeed, Bonnie corroborated that Spaghetti, one of the original Irish Volunteers, had made amends with his archenemies from the Apprentice Boys of Derry, including a number of them that he had assisted in transitioning to the higher realm. They even play Hurling together, so anything is possible, although I could see where the idea of rapidly swinging club-like bats in close proximity to thick Celtic skulls would have its appeal with even the most forgiving Irishman. Nonetheless, just when I thought I had witnessed every conceivable miracle, receiving a supporting message from the mafia hitman that once killed me, certainly recalibrated my standards for unbelievable.

There are no hard feelings in heaven, Jimmy. Bobbi confirmed. *Dan says he has a weekly card game with Valachi and your brothers – and he does not even care that the Ginger likes to cheat at poker.*

Despite how it turned out, the truth of the matter was that prior to entering the Witness Protection Program, Dan might have been the one true friend I had in the world. And the real irony was that the last time I had to "go to the mattresses" was when Valachi and Dan had come to Berthoud to kill me and my family.

As I reviewed today's encounter from my enhanced perspective, as well as that borrowed from everyone else at the table that morning, Grimm Twin Seth had given up way too easy on the Toyota identification, especially since the image of my tax return being shared with Victor demonstrated that Seth knew I was full of shit. And if that was not enough, Gina's field stripping show-and-tell using their weapons at the end of our sit down, demonstrated that the Pink Pony Girl they were so interested in was just an appetizer on the menu from the paranormal-preternatural-extraterrestrial smorgasbord. It also showed Seth and his flip side that we were not going to roll over at their techno-demigod act. We were the real thing and that was a threat to their self-realized omnipotence. Their conjoined, megalomaniacal ego would never stand for that.

Dan's message from beyond the veil was plain and simple. The Grimm Twins would be back with reinforcements, and we better be ready for them.

CHAPTER THIRTY-NINE
(Scouting Reports)

The last time I was part of a war council, the internet chatter picked up by Lenahan's friends in the government told us Valachi's team was coming to Berthoud with their biggest bats to play baseball.

I was the rookie on that ballistic baseball team, and I batted ninth in the order on a roster of only six players and two reserves.

Given their well-honed and field-tested skillset with weapons, Eddie and Lenny alternately batted first, second, third and fourth in the order. Bobbi, with her magical control over nature, pinch hit at number five, and ultimately hit the walk off home run against Valachi's team. Helen and Gina, both with a demonstrated naturally aggressive proficiency around firearms, switched off at sixth and seventh and Claire, the true dark mule with her own psychic abilities and deadly physical strength, batted eighth in the line-up. Everett and Michelle, the two biggest bats on the team, were relegated, due to then existing Centaurian rules, to observer status, functioning as the team's coach and manager. And we still gutted out a win against a well-trained, modern-day Murderer's Row.

This time, our team was stacked like the '96 Yankees. Eddie and Lenny had been fortified on the ballistic front by Whitey, who also brought his preternatural abilities as a werewolf into the mix. Everett and Michelle had cleared themselves to play on a fully extraterrestrial level. Gina and I had been given serious physical and telepathic upgrades in our Tellurian-Centaurian hybrid makeovers and remained relatively proficient with handguns. Claire's strength and telepathy that had proven invaluable during the last outing, had only improved through the cross-pollination with the rest of us. Helen remained a solid human utility player who knew her way around a handgun and Bobbi still had her magic. Eileen was an unknown but could be subbed into pinch hit, and I could tell she would take one for the team if she had to. Finally, we had two promising young prospects in Stella and Apollo, but they were still paying their dues at the Triple A level, and I had no intentions of calling them up to the majors for this series. To top it all off, most of our team could access the opposing team's signals, so we knew every pitch they were throwing.

And where the two brothers could also communicate telepathically, in that strange twin-speak, theirs was a closed, technology-based, circuit, and they were the only two on the line. Although, from the looks of things, their Cas-Lux AI enhancement may have extended the reach of their communication system, it still was limited to sharing information between the twin hosts. Our communication system, on the other hand, was built around a core of enhanced biological circuitry light years ahead of its human counterpart, that made T-Mobile's 5-G cell phone network look like a couple of orange juice cans connected by string. Those of us with the gift, original or upgraded, could freely communicate with each other in real time, and most could also tap into the minds of our purely human teammates and opponents. One of our team mates could sometimes peek at tomorrow's boxscores. Our eyes were everywhere. So, when the announcement came for a cleanup in aisle seven, we had the mops, and the twins would be the mess.

The Grimm Twins had been given a slight scouting advantage when they saw Gina's batting practice and got a look at Eddie and Lenny taking their cuts in the on-deck circle. That ex-spook, BC, might even have gotten a peak at Whitey in the upstairs owner's box. All we saw were a couple of wealthy, twin asshole team owners, who had a core of functional utility infielders but had the unlimited resources and brains to buy the best free agents on the market. And they were not coming back to play until they had put together their all-star team.

So that left us with the one advantage that would never change. When they finally came, they were going to play on our home field, and we were a seasoned group of extremely talented players with an unbeaten record, who were not playing for our owner's money, but for each other.

CHAPTER FORTY
(Circling the Wagons)

Just like during the period immediately following Apollo's birth, the core of misfits returned to the extended Casa Moran compound. Bobbi and Helen moved into the spare bedroom at Everett and Michelle's home. Eileen took over our basement, which allowed her to turn the kitchenette into a makeshift medical emergency station. Eddie rotated between The Oracle and our home, bunking each night in the upgraded *Two Mule Salon* out in the back property. Some nights, he would invite Claire through the oversized doorway of the refurbished studio for long talks about the horrors he experienced during the war. I knew from experience how remedial those conversations with Claire could be, as she was the wisest among us. Lenny's government job required his absence during most daylight hours, but he always stopped in at the end of each day to check in on us and Maeve, who had been bunking with Blue for the duration. Lenny remained in constant contact by cell phone when physically separated. Whitey spent most daylight hours circulating between our two properties but spent each night in feral form, roaming the surrounding woods and fields, looking for anything that might be a threat.

Eddie, Lenny, and Whitey also secluded themselves in the Salon accumulating and prepping a cache of armaments, including long guns and their accessories. They would often throw a collection of them into the back of Lenny's SUV and drive off to his range in the Boulder mountains for a few hours of fun and firearms.

The crew continued their home schooling of the children, which was a great distraction for us all, but Michelle spent the most time in their presence during their waking hours teaching them every little trick she knew. This allowed me to keep one eye on Michelle, given Bobbi's prognostication that they would come for our most powerful first.

Claire continued to be the children's outdoor nanny and kept a vigilant eye on them whenever they were playing outdoors. For added security, Whitey, Eddie, or Lenny, sat out on the back deck with a long gun whenever the children were outside.

Everett kept an eye on the twins, which included a few fleeting flyovers of their Baker, Oregon compound. Everett's repeated reconnaissance disclosed that there was a steady increase in the number of humans circulating on the property, as well as the appearance of some heavy-duty construction machinery, but concluded that all of the work must have been being performed below the existing structures on the property. After his first foray, he determined that the twins had installed a sophisticated radar system and so he had to keep his flyovers at a high enough altitude to avoid being spotted.

Gina managed the team and made sure everyone had whatever they needed and that everyone stayed in regular contact with each other. She also hosted all of the daily meals.

I funded the entire operation and ensured that we, as a group and as individuals, had whatever resources we needed to survive, thrive, and prepare during this waiting period. I also used all of my enhanced skills to keep building my fortune. In an abundance of caution, I also retained a high-powered East Coast Trusts and Estates Lawyer named John Vaughan, who had attended Fordham Law School with me during my Jimmy McCarthy days, to oversee and maintain the labyrinthian web of Jimmy Moran's and Mark Wallen's offshore trusts, financial and securities accounts, including those based in Gibraltar, in the event I was no longer able to do it. He stood out as a decent human being among the sharks in our class. I introduced myself over the phone as Mark Wallen, trust fund scion, and as soon as my substantial retainer cleared, we were off to the races. I figured if he was bright and savvy enough to be retained by some of the more prominent attendees of the World Economic Forum's annual Davos-

Kloster consortium, he could handle my affairs. With any luck, I was hoping to never have to call upon his retainer.

So, the days and weeks trickled forward like Groundhog Day with the Sword of Damocles still hanging over our heads. I did not need Bobbi's soothsaying skills to know that sooner or later, the Grimm Twins would come for us. And finally, they did.

CHAPTER FORTY-ONE
(Eye in the Sky)

As a local contractor and employer, Whitey was such a regular fixture in town that it made the most sense for him to be the one to keep an ear to the ground there. He could pop into the Ace Hardware store or any of the coffee shops or restaurants and just listen to the regulars share their topical observations of the comings and goings around town. And there was nothing more notable in a small town than a strange face.

But Whitey had nothing new to report. The attention of Carl and his crew of morning regulars at Grandpa's Café were fixed on the continued battle between the various state licensing authorities and the local establishments that refused to submit to their draconian pandemic edicts. Similarly, the afternoon crowd playing darts and quaffing beers at Side Tracked, made no reference to a return of the metrosexuals that had caused such a stir right after the Pink Pony Girl event.

Maybe Gina scared them off? Whitey pondered.

* * * * *

Everett was the first to notice the eye in the sky. We were both sitting in parallel chase lounges on the back deck during the early morning hours, sipping some wine and watching the October starscape. Whitey was out in feral form on his regular nocturnal security check. Lenny had stopped by for a quick meal and then taken Maeve and Blue back to his digs for a change of scenery. The rest of the humans had all turned in for the night, although the lights in the Two Mule Salon meant Eddie and Claire were still sharing one of their deeper philosophical discussions about the meaning of life and death out there on the back property. That Claire was one hell of a good listener. Gina and Michelle had just dematerialized to pop into the children's rooms to check on Apollo and Stella. I was channeling my best four-year-old while counting the dozens of overhead satellites crossing from all points on the compass. My count was sometimes interrupted by the beautiful streak of a solitary meteorite and my corresponding "Wow!" It all brought back memories of how bright the Northern Colorado starscape first appeared to Gina and me on our first night in Berthoud. What seemed like only yesterday was millions of miles ago.

Space seemed less foreign to me since my visit to Proxima Centauri b. I thought for a moment about the beauty and cuteness of Petrichor and Dr. Nim, respectively, and then, to get myself off of that mental track, recalled the moment I broke Aldor's nose. Everett, who had been hitching a ride on my thoughts, laughed at the last memory.

"To good times!" he said while clinking my glass in a toast.

Then we both spotted a string of approximately thirty satellites passing overhead from Northwest to Southeast. It was 3 a.m.

That Elon Musk is a visionary. Everett shared. *By funding that SpaceX venture he has singlehandedly cut a third off the time before humanity enters into the Galactic Federation.*

"To Elon Musk!" I said, this time clinking Everett's wine glass. "And his Starlink satellites."

We continued to watch as the last of the satellite string crossed over our heads.

"We should take Jayney out for an up close and personal look at them," he said with the slightest slur in his speech. I looked over at the three empty bottles of Charles Krug Cab-Sav we had killed that evening and wondered if you could get a DWI in space.

"Maybe tomorrow." I suggested. At this point the last of that Starlink string was just crossing the apex of the star canopy.

Look, a straggler. Everett shared, pointing at a single light that seemed to come from the Northwest and follow along the Starlink flight path a second later. We watched as it quickly closed the distance on the last of the string before it. And just as it was arriving directly over our heads it slowed dramatically, almost coming to a complete stop, allowing the Starlink string to continue on without it.

"That's weird," Everett said, studying the object. "Don't know any of earth's satellite technology that could do that." And after a second or two of almost hovering overhead, the object started to accelerate and quickly caught up to and fell in place at the end of the Starlink string just before it disappeared over the southern horizon.

Tomorrow we fly. Everett shared.

CHAPTER FORTY-TWO
(Going Hunting)

The next midnight found Everett and I sitting back at Jayney's holographic control panels. I would be lying if I did not admit that I found Jayney's rendition of Petrichor's voice just a little bit titillating as she took us through the final prep for takeoff. I was still not comfortable bringing the car out of the garage and driveway, so Everett took us from launch to the edge of the atmosphere. And it is just as well that he did because we were no sooner airborne then we were approached by two F-16 Fighting Falcons from the 140th Fighter Group at Buckley Airforce Base. I would love to say that I identified the craft and their squadron, but I just lifted that information from Everett's worried mind once Jayney alerted us to their approach.

I have noticed that your new government has been increasing its military presence in the area, including ground troops, Everett shared nonchalantly as he made a right-hand turn that lost our trackers, who continued past us at Mach 2, before accelerating at a ninety-degree ascent that took us into an orbit at what Jayney explained was approximately 342 miles above the earth. It was like a couple of bicycles chasing a Ferrari. I was really getting the hang of this space travel. I did not even feel any butterflies from Everett's evasive maneuvers. Once Everett positioned us directly above the Berthoud homestead, he turned the control of the space craft over to Jayney.

Maintain our present position. He instructed her.

"Now we wait." He said as our holographic chairs pulled away from the panel and the outer skin of the spaceship disappeared, which gave me a fleeting sensation that I was about to fall through the bottom of the craft.

Despite sitting above the North American Continent, the earth maintained its beautiful blue luster, no doubt due to the fact that about 70 percent of the planet is covered with water, a fact I was aware of all on my own.

Shit, is that Michelle waiving up at us? I shared. I could not believe Everett looked.

Are you going to do this all night? He asked.

I can't help it; space travel makes me giddy. I responded truthfully.

We kept ourselves entertained by watching a number of satellites pass across the same orbit, a few passing too close to Jayney for my comfort. I remember my mother was a terrible back seat driver when I first procured my driver's license at the precious age of seventeen. Mom tended to whistle quite audibly every time a car came anywhere close to ours as I sped along the streets. Now the cars all come with built in motion sensors that serve the same purpose. I whistled a few times that night while sitting in Jayney.

Everett really impressed me by being able to name not only the model and type of satellites that passed, but also rattle off a whole lot of technical details that soon became white noise in my brain. *Nerds.*

Finally, Jayney alerted us to the pending advance of the string of sixty satellites approaching from behind us. I was not sure what I expected but the first thing I noticed about these satellites was that they each looked like a silvery motherboard from a computer. Every satellite was long and flat, about the width and length of a small car. Each had a long flat set of solar panels extending like a sail from the side facing away from the earth. They invoked the image of a Lego windsurf board.

Jayney appeared to lift us further away from the earth to allow this string of satellites to pass directly underneath us. Up close they appeared to pass in a zipper formation with every other satellite following two close and parallel trajectories. After about thirty seconds the trailing last of the identical Starlink satellites passed by.

Wait for it! Everette declared.

Coming up the rear at that same accelerated pace displayed last night was a smaller rectangular object that appeared quite different from the ones before it. It was an ugly duckling behind a string of swans.

Everett pointed down at the passing object. "Watch this."

Grab that one Jayney. Everett commanded. Jayney started to accelerate until it matched the speed of the object below it. Then a beam shot out from some spot in Jayney's belly, locked onto the object and drew it through the spacecraft's invisible skin and into the interior space directly below our invisible floor. I kept waiting for all of the oxygen in the cabin to go rushing out of Jayney like a torn balloon.

"You have a tractor beam?" I said, amazed once again.

"Jayney has lots of toys I haven't shown you yet." Everett responded.

I continued to stare down at the object in the bay below us. It started to vibrate and glow like it was pissed off.

"That's not going to blow up, is it?" I asked.

"Shit, I hope not," Everett deadpanned aurally. "Take us home, Jayney."

CHAPTER FORTY-THREE
(Peeping Twins)

The return flight, as all return trips do, seemed to be faster than the trip out into space, so before we knew it, Everett was maneuvering Jayney carefully through the large bay door that opened on the back of the building housing Everett's mancave. Strangely enough, Everett had never invited me into this space before. He had always retrieved and replaced Jayney on his own. Even Centaurian males needed their sanctuary.

Shit, I wish I still had the Hadron Distributor. Everett shared in frustration as he now eased the full-sized craft through the RV doorway and set it down gently next to a smaller model the size of a minivan, which Everett had once explained was for emergency use only as Michelle's escape vehicle in the event that Everett was killed or captured during one of his forays wrangling some of earth's more problematic space efforts. The smaller craft looked pristine. I wondered what Michelle called it.

Once we exited Jayney, I expected to see some large, futuristic workstation at the far end of this building where Everett was going to dismantle and analyze the snatched satellite, but instead there was a simple wooden worktable with a lot of run-of-the-mill human tools on it. Before I could ask him about it, he commanded "Report please, Jayney."

Jayney digitally downloaded her full analysis of the satellite to both of our brains in a few seconds, but most of the technical information was completely lost on me. What I did retain was that the satellite had enhanced video capability more sophisticated than the Hubble telescope that could read the time on a man's watch on the earth below. It also had infrared sensors that could identify warm blooded creatures within the buildings it scanned and could transmit this information to a receiver back on earth at 500 Mbps, by transmitting it digitally through the string of proceeding Starlink satellites it had accessed in an almost parasitic fashion.

Jayney shared a copy of a series of digital videos that had been recorded since its launch as part of the Starlink payload just the week before. After scanning it at Centaurian speed we were privy to recordings of the Moran version of The Truman Show. Unfortunately for us, those videos captured various members of the crew dematerializing and transporting through heat signature movement in and between the various buildings and barn, including those smaller signatures belonging to Stella and Apollo. It also captured heat signatures moving between my place and the home of Everett and Michelle. Fortunately, it did not capture Whitey transforming, before or after his nightly woodland circuit, since he always began and completed his tour from his home, which was a quarter mile down Beverly Drive and out of the satellite camera's path.

The most important information that Jayney downloaded was that the satellite's circuitry bore nano-sized laser inscriptions of the logo of G2N. Those twins must have paid someone a lot of money to stowaway their spy satellite in that Falcon 9 rocket as part of the Starlink payload. And now they had our roster and a real time scouting report.

CHAPTER FORTY-FOUR
(Raising the Stakes)

"What if they get the government involved?" Lenny asked before he sucked down an entire mug of coffee. "I'm not going to be able to bury that." He looked exhausted, and rightfully so. I had literally snatched him out of his bed and transported him back to the compound as soon as Jayney had finished downloading her report. I never pegged him for the Star Wars geek his pajamas suggested.

"No," Everett responded. "The Grimm Twins consider themselves above any government. The government comes to them and their techno-brahmans for help."

I took a peek into Everett's mind and the date, November 4, 2020, flashed for a moment. Everett obviously cared far more than I did about the world he had adopted.

"So, what do we do now?" Whitey asked.

"You have to go!" Eileen said to Gina. "Take the kids back to England."

Eileen's right, Claire seconded from out in the yard. *You have to protect the young ones.*

"Yes, go!" Eddie added. "We got your six."

I had exposed my original blood family to enough danger for a human lifetime and paid the price by getting my brothers killed. The Grimm Twins had shown they were as serious in their pursuit of their prey as Valachi. How hard would it be for their Cas-Lux AI to track us across the earth? I was not going to expose Bonnie and Tessa to that, and I was not going to run and leave my new family behind to clean up my mess.

"Spirit says it ends here." Bobbi murmured, eyes closed, her head nestled on Helen's shoulder as the two rested on the couch in the living room. I thought they had both fallen back to sleep after Michelle transported them to our house.

"Spirit's right, we're not going anywhere!" Gina stated defiantly. "I'm tired of running away from chickenshit assholes, and that's what these two little douchebags are, a couple of oversized brains wrapped in the bullying power of their money and technology. Well, we have money too, and our technology whips theirs' ass."

"Fucking right!" Michelle added.

"I gotta get me a Centaurian woman!" Lenny shouted.

"I hope she has a sister." Whitey added.

"So, what's the next move?" Eileen asked.

* * * * *

Fifteen minutes later Michelle maneuvered Jayney into a low orbit and shared the coordinates: *44° 46' 30" N / 117° 50' 0" W*. As we were heading northwest, the night was still before us.

Michelle demonstrated a lot more natural confidence at Jayney's holographic control panel than her spouse. That included showing a lot more balls when another pair of F-16s chased us across the Northern Colorado sky and into Wyoming. Michelle was clearly enjoying herself and waited until Jayney alerted us to the bogeys having their weapons locked on before taking evasive action and leaving them in the dust with a "Whoop!" She did not even bother engaging the plasma shield or exiting the atmosphere until we had reached Idaho. By then, all ten knuckles on my hands were white. MUFON was going to have a field day.

Are we sure we want to do this? Everett asked, from his holographic chair on the other side of his standing spouse. He was clearly not used to being second in command on this ship.

The vote was unanimous back at the house. I responded from my spot off to Michelle's right side. *Even you put up your hand.*

That was your high-test coffee talking. Everett responded.

Boys, boys, not now, Momma needs to concentrate. Michelle reprimanded.

Over Baker, Oregon. Jayney shared a moment later.

"Hang on to your hats!" Michelle shouted as she moved her fingers like Rachmaninov across the controls and took Jayney into a nosedive. Despite the plasma shield, I felt my stomach drop.

We came in low over the Wallowa Mountain range, skimming the treetops along the edge of Eagle Cap Mountain, then headed directly towards the Grimm Twins compound.

Radar detected. Jayney shared.

Good, Michelle responded, *I want them to know we are coming.*

Michelle homed in on the area where the large construction machinery was parked just as the Klieg lights on their compound lit up the area like JFK at night.

Let her rip, Jayney! Michelle commanded.

The walls and floor of the ship disappeared and the three of us watched as Jayney jettisoned the GN2 satellite from her belly. It propelled through the air like a large silver surfboard and crashed head on into the side of a two-story concrete building that was still under construction in the far corner of the compound. It took a one Mississippi count before the flames erupted through the concrete roof top. Michelle inverted the spacecraft so we could get a better look at the explosion as we passed over the building. I was waiting for my lovely long locks to singe, but we were gone before the flames reached us.

Oh, I wish Gina could have seen that! Michelle shared.

Loved every second of it! Gina piped in from the ether. *I got Jimmy's eye view.*

I'm never going to learn to put that toilet seat down.

Take us home, Jayney! Michelle commanded. *Message delivered.*

CHAPTER FORTY-FIVE
(DEFCON 1: White Alert)

The government's DEFCON System for threat assessment reduces in numbers from five to one as the level of intensity and preparedness rises from a perceived to imminent threat. As Eddie was explaining to the group the morning after Michelle's special delivery, we had reached a level of DEFCON 1, known in military parlance as "Cocked Pistol" and whose color code is "White," not the more blood invoking "Red" that is bandied about in modern fiction. As Eddie explained to the gathering, since the DEFCON system's creation in 1957, the U.S. government has never raised the status of the country's military to DEFCON 1, and I was shocked to learn that it only raised the threat level to DEFCON 3, on September 11th, 2001. I did not have to wonder what kind of threat to my family I needed to feel before cocking my pistol, Michelle's special delivery to the Grimm Twins was a declaration of war.

Fighting sucks on every level, from school yard to battlefield and, if you are smart, you will avoid it at all costs. No one has ever accused me of being smart.

The Grimm Twins were either shocked by the audacity of our response and decided that discretion really is the better part of valor and backed off, or they were dumber than they looked and were just regrouping and upping their game. Turns out it was the latter.

So, we went to the mattresses. Lenny and Whitey, and their massive number of collective armaments, moved into the Two Mule Salon with Eddie. Claire repeatedly walked the perimeter of the property every night from dusk to dawn until she wore down the high grass along the fence line into a smooth clay bridle path. Only when the humans were awake to take over her watch did she lie down in the field beside Mr. Rogers' gravesite to sleep for a few hours. Feral Whitey performed his one-mile perimeter rotation each night before bedding down and then shared the perimeter day watch with Lenny and Eddie. Each night, Everett stood watch on the back deck area mostly staring up into space and I sat on the front porch, my back to the front door, avoiding boredom by alternating counting the posts along the front fence line, fifty to be exact, engaging in a staring contest with Jack the Spruce, I always lost, and finally reciting the names that went with the multi-colored row of hats on gnome hill. The males had received the more British sounding, whimsical names, Geoffrey, Tristan, Felix, Addison, Carlyle, Sinjin, and Edmund, the female gnomes were more Americanized and only answered to Terry, Jeanne, Maureen, Anne, and Mary. Felix was the worst-assed looking of the bunch, as his pointed gnome hat still bore the scar of the first bullet meant for me the night of the Storm.

Colorado in October was enjoying an Indian Summer, so sweatshirts were sufficient to maintain outdoor comfort. We left the top floor windows and the rear facing sliding deck doors open to allow the cool night air to circulate through the house for the comfort of those that needed sleep.

Michelle and Gina alternated sitting watch in each of the children's' rooms. Helen and Bobbi stayed in the Tower, slept at night, and ran the kitchen throughout the day. Eileen slept in the basement at night, first aid kit at the ready, but converted her area into a functioning home school for Apollo and Stella during daylight hours. The telepathically gifted continued to check in on on another regularly during our night watch.

To tell you the truth, after the first week it was fucking boring.

By week two, Everett began running night reconnaissance missions in Jayney over the Grimm Twins' Baker, Oregon property. He reported telepathically in real time about the massive buildup of construction activity repairing the demolished bunker as well as an increased number of land vehicles around the bunk house. The most disturbing information shared was that each time Jayney attempted to scan the property for any intelligence, she was met and diverted by their Cas-Lux AI and a moment later would receive a radar ping and be forced into evasive measures by a reading that some ground-based weapon had locked onto their position.

The Grimm Twins had added a CH-47 Chinook Twin Engine Helicopter to their toy collection and modified their Sikorsky S-92 with twin rods jutting out of each side. From Everett's perspective, all of the upgrades looked defensive.

By the end of week three, with Halloween fast approaching, we had started to convince ourselves that the Grimm Twins had given up. We maintained our prophylactic security measures, but you could tell that everyone, including myself, were quietly issuing respective sighs of relief and dropping our guard just a little. Wishful thinking. That was the last big mistake we ever made.

CHAPTER FORTY-SIX
(The Last Halloween)

Bobbi was in her element on Halloween, or Samhain, as she liked to call it. She distracted us during our dinner meal around the table with her stories, all told aurally for the maximum dramatic effect, about her family's paranormal lineage going back hundreds of years. She performed simple feats of natural magik, made orbs dance through the air and had Stella demonstrate her growing mastery of the Fairy King's Diamond. The kids carved pumpkins and set them in the front windows, with tea light candles inside, but there were no trick-or-treaters. Just friendly ghosts. The goblins showed up the next night once the last fingernail of the moon had disappeared.

* * * * *

I sat at my front porch post, counting gnome hats and fenceposts to kill the time while listening to the haunting sound of the warning horn from the BNSF freight train heading north past all of the local railway crossings. I was thankful that its railway line ran ten miles to the east, closer to the town of Berthoud. I could not imagine being a townie trying to sleep through that sound, assuming I needed to sleep at all.

Jimmy, come quick, something is happening. Everett pleaded.

I was at his side on the back deck before he had completed his thought and found him pointing toward the back of the property. The moonless night was pitch, and I could still hear the horns of the freight train as it made it past the last few crossings in the distance. As my eyes adjusted, I could see the movement of suddenly disturbed birds and bats fluttering *en mass* from their nests and boxes into the night sky across the back property, before they each started to fall motionless to the ground. Eddie, Lenny, and Whitey flew out of the Two Mule Salon, guns in hand, wearing nothing but their skivvies. None of them made it more than a few steps before collapsing.

Jimmy, help me. Claire's panicked, sultry voice entered my mind just as I spotted her large shadow running full gallop in our direction towards the backyard fence. She leapt into the air and cleared the fence, only to land limp and lifeless onto the hard earth below her. She continued sliding forward another ten feet, her huge mass gouging the earth as a trail. Before I could move to her side, Everett sniffed and then shouted "Carfentanil," before collapsing onto the deck beside me.

I turned back towards the sliding doors in an effort to close them, but my entire body went numb, and I fell to the deck flipping over on my back as I did so. I landed hard, facing the night sky. And there I saw the outline of the Grimm Twins black chopper, hovering above the house with a thick dark mist billowing from numerous spouts on the bottom of the extended rods on either side of its body. The rotating blades were forcing the mist downward. I watched, helplessly, as it pooled on the deck around me while also entering through the doors and through the upper open windows.

I cannot move, shared Gina.

What's happening? Michelle added, trying to mask her fear.

We've been drugged by Carfentanil. Everett responded. *The humans are out cold, not even dreaming.*

What about the kids? I asked, amazed that I was subdued but fully conscious.

Comatose. Michelle shared, and I could see from her viewpoint that Stella was motionless in her bed.

Same here, Gina added, sharing her visual of the unconscious Apollo. I studied the movement of their chests just to be sure they were breathing.

Claire! I reached out to her but there was no response.

Down for the count, Everett shared. *I can see her lying in the backyard, but she's breathing.*

I scanned both houses and everyone was incapacitated to various degrees.

All I could do was stare straight up towards the sky. Not one of the voluntary muscles in my body functioned. But my brain was working, and I could connect with the other adult Centauri and hybrids.

I scanned the pilot of the overhead chopper. It was Colonel Dzikas. He was at that moment reporting by radio transmission to the Grimm Twins back in Baker, Oregon.

"Bringing in the squad now. "

"Careful with the girl." I could hear Seth's voice coming through the chopper radio as Dzika listened.

I was distracted by the sound of a new set of propellers.

Another chopper. The Chinook. Everett shared. *It's landing out back.*

Everett shared his view of the huge, two-rotor, machine as it touched down on the back field and then twelve heavily armed men exited and made their way quickly towards the house. I recognize the mental patterns from the three security members who were now leading the others.

One stopped outside the Salon and checked the vitals of each of the fallen, and then moved on.

The stream of black clad warriors wearing protective facial gear and carrying long guns flowed silently past the unconscious Claire and then below the deck and into the basement. A moment later, a man appeared and straddled my body. He was dressed in black and wore a synthetic mask that covered his entire face. I could make out the etching of a model number on the side of the mask. It had a clear visor that displayed everything above the nose line. It had dual air filters on either jowl, and I could hear the sound of the sucking air as he stood there above me.

It was the tall skinny one they called BC. He reached down and placed two fingers of his latex covered hand on my carotid artery.

"Out cold," BC called into his shoulder clip radio. He reached over and checked Everett. "So is the other one."

"Good," came the voice of Colonel Dzikas from the radio. "Complete the mission. See you back at Baker." I watched as the silent black chopper disappeared over the house.

"Found the girl," said another voice in response. "Still out cold. She looks older than the photo."

"Take her to the chopper." Dzikas barked.

I'm going to kill you! Michelle's voice blasted in our heads as she watched, helpless and paralyzed, as the one called "Carl," lifted Stella from her bed and exited the room.

I heard the voices of other men chiming in as they found and marked the rest of the people inside the house. One mentioned finding two dogs out cold under the dining room table. BC acknowledged each man in turn.

"We've found another kid." Another voice came across BC's radio. "A boy. Looks like the girl, but younger. Out for the count."

Stay away from my son! Shrieked the equally compromised Gina a moment later. This time I could see the one called Disco, standing over Apollo.

"Take him too." BC responded over the radio. "Everyone else, back to the chopper. We're done here."

"What about the dark-haired bitch?" Disco called into the radio as he gestured towards Gina. "That gun she destroyed cost me five grand."

"Leave her," BC responded. "We're here for the children. No freelancing."

Aaaaaggggghhhhh!!!! I could hear the pain in Gina's telepathic transmission as I watched her view of Disco lifting Apollo and carrying him out of the room.

Jimmy, look. Everett shared.

I shifted to Everett's viewpoint. Claire was gone.

CHAPTER FORTY-SEVEN
(One More Ghost)

I scanned for Claire and found her mind confused and fuzzy, as she tried to regain control of her body. I could see through her eyes that she was standing under the rear deck, back in the corner by the alcove for the hot tub. She was leaning her body weight against the building. She in turn was scanning our minds and was fixed on the latest messages from Michelle and Gina concerning the kidnapping of Stella and Apollo. I could tell that she was shaking her head trying to bring some clarity, and she then focused her eyes on the sliding back doors.

At that moment one of the mercenaries exited the house and stepped to the left of the basement doorway, scanning the area, while extending his right arm across the doorway as a visual bar to whomever was following. He looked over at Claire with little interest and reported into his radio.

"The mule is back on her feet so the rest may be coming to soon."

"Better wrap it up." Came Dzika's reply across the radio.

As the mercenary turned to look back through the doorway, I could see Claire closing the distance.

"Hey, asshole?" She hissed.

The man's surprised look at the sound of Claire's sultry voice turned to horror as her right front hoof came slamming down on his head with the sound of a cantaloupe on concrete. As Carl Serrano followed through the sliding door he spotted his dead comrade and immediately raised the limp body of Stella before him as a shield. I could see Claire drop her cocked hoof in frustration while physically cornering him and threatening, "Put her down you fucker!"

I did not see the muzzle flash, but I heard the clacking sound of the muffled report, and I felt the impact and agony that Claire experienced in real time as the 7.62 NATO rounds from the AR-10 ripped into the left side of her chest and neck, driving her thousand-pound body to her right, sending her crashing through the double glass sliding doors.

Every telepathic mind in the house shrieked in unison at the image. It was the sound of the Banshee.

Jim. . . Jim . . .Jimmy. . . . I could feel the pain in Claire's thoughts. *I'm. . . sorry.*

Claire barely lifted her head out of the twisted metal and shards of broken glass and gazed back in the direction of her assaulter. The asshole BC now stood over the fallen mule and examined the damage his still smoking weapon had done with the emotionless detachment of his psychopathy. Bored, he looked up and waved the others out of the darkness, past her body and back into the night. He stopped only to lift and toss the dead body of his fallen comrade across his shoulder with the care of a trash man.

I could hear Claire's heartbreaking, faint, whinnies rising from below us. I focused everything I had into recovering some movement, but the paralysis remained. I could not even scream, but tears were flowing from my eyes and soaking the hair beside my ears.

Claire, just hang in there for me. I begged.

Claire, honey, hang on. Gina cried.

I'm so sorry Jimmy. Claire shared, her vision darkening, her view staring at the glass shards on the floor before her lowered head. I could barely make out the reflection of her eye in the glass directly beneath her head. Her blood was everywhere. Seeping from her mouth. *I tried to stop them.*

Rest darling. I answered, focusing all of my energy in her direction.

I'm cold, Jimmy. Claire shared, and I shivered in response to the chill she was experiencing. I raised the images of our time together from the first moment I spotted her on the Reynolds farm. I wanted her to feel the love that I had for her as she lay alone in the darkness below me. She shared some others of hers in return, the time I freed her from the fence, the time she scared the shit out of me in the dark of her Lair, but the images started to fade.

I love you Claire, stay with me.

I love you Jimmy, . . . and Gina, . . . and the kids. Claire's thoughts and corresponding images were slowing. Her breathing was labored. I tried again to move my body.

Jimmy . . . I gotta go now. . . it's Mr. Rogers. . . he's here . . .

I heard Claire take her last breath in the darkness below, and then release.

The sound of the now firing Chinook engine drew my attention to Everett's viewpoint as the large twin prop machine lifted skyward, kicking up the red dust while bending the high grass. I followed its ascent for as long as it remained in Everett's unmoving frame. I have never felt such hatred course through my body or felt so impotent.

My mind bayed with an anguish that no creature could give voice to.

The sudden impact of the others' responsive telepathic pain was too much for me to bare and the last images I recalled was the face of BC, first as he stood over me, and then over Claire, then blackness took me.

CHAPTER FORTY-EIGHT
(First Bury The Dead)

I was awakened with a hard slap, the kind that torques your face 90 degrees and leaves a handprint for at least a half hour.

"Jimmy. . . Jimmy . . . wake the fuck up."

Through my haze I recognized Michelle's voice and my mind responded.

The fluttering of my eyelids confirmed to me that I was recovering the control over my body. The next thing I felt were my fingers stretching out to provide me some leverage to lift myself into a leaning position on one elbow as I tried to get my bearings. Michelle appeared carrying Gina and set her down on the deck, leaning her up against a nearby wall. Gina was slowly recovering consciousness as well.

Are you all right? Gina whispered.

I went to reply aurally, but my throat was parched, and I could not get the words out.

I think so, I responded telepathically, *a hell of a headache. You?*

My lungs are burning, but I think I'm okay. Gina replied.

I looked over to the empty space where Everett had fallen.

We both recovered on our own about a half hour ago. Michelle entered my thoughts. *You guys just started to stir. Everett found some Narcan in Lenny's red-cross bag and is administering it to the others. So far, they are all recovering.*

Then the nightmare returned. *Claire?*

I started to stand up, but it was at human speed, and I was still so woozy that I had to lean on the deck railing for support.

Michelle steadied me, then pulled me into a hug.

"She's gone, Jimmy." Michelle whispered. "Hours before we woke up."

I dematerialized away from Michelle's arms and appeared below deck, staring down at the body of my fallen friend and mentor, bloody and broken. The deep, howling sound that rose up out of my chest was not human, and shredded my burning vocal cords as it escaped. A moment later, I heard a similar sound coming from the back.

I'm so sorry, Jimmy. Whitey shared as the Narcan kicked in.

I cleared some glass with my foot and knelt beside Claire's face. Her deep brown eyes were still open, and her long black lashes were still beautiful. But her body was cold, her mind still, her life force long gone.

Weeping, I closed her eyes with my fingertips, lifted her head in my hands and kissed her softly on her snout, searching desperately for some semblance of that connection we had so deeply shared these past few years. I just could not say goodbye. Could not let her go. I felt so alone. I buried my face into the soft, cold fur of her neck and felt the stiffness of her blood-soaked mane. All emotions just released, the tears flowed, and I sobbed in a manner I had not experienced since the death of my brothers. My body shook and I could not catch my breath.

I felt a hand on my shoulder and looked up to see Gina, crying openly as she tried to comfort me. I rose to her embrace and we both just stood there, rocking in each other's arms. I could not get my mind to start working. I was lost in my own despair.

"We need to bury Claire." Came Lenahan's somber voice from behind us. "Whitey's gone for his backhoe."

"No," I said, wiping my face on my sleeve. "I've got this."

I transported to my toolshed and grabbed one of the Lesche long handled spades, then transported out back to the spot beside Mr. Rogers' gravesite and started to dig manually. I worked at full Centaurian speed and in ten minutes, stood, exhausted for the first time since my transformation, in the bottom of a large pit. Gina suddenly appeared carrying the comforter, quilt, and pillows from our king-sized bed. She spread the comforter on the ground and placed the pillows gently at the Northern end of this ditch, directly across from where the head of Mr. Rogers lay buried in the grave beside us.

"Go get her," Gina whispered.

I transported back to the house and found that Michelle had cleared away all of the glass and washed the blood from Claire's fur. Bobbi, Helen, Eileen, Eddie, Lenny, and Whitey were standing above Claire in honor guard formation. They each looked like they had been through hell.

"She's fine," Bobbi whispered, "Claire and Mr. Rogers are wandering through the Elysium Fields with Spaghetti. She's met the Junkie and his mule."

I smiled weakly at the thought of my grandfather and that spry little friend of his.

"Junkie just said, *Bheir sinn deagh aire don*," Bobbi repeated.

"We'll take good care of the lassie." Everett translated for the crowd.

"Junkie's mule, whose name is Sara, said you were a terror when you were a 'wee leanbh'."

"Child." Everett repeated in English.

"Claire just said its time to put her body to rest." Bobbi continued, "You've got to get those kids."

I was so lost in my own agony; I had forgotten the children. I knelt down and, rocking Claire's body onto her back, I reached underneath her and with a strength I had never tested, lifted her thousand pounds effortlessly into the air. I transported us to the grave, knelt and placed her gently on the comforter. Gina arranged Claire's head facing Mr. Rogers' grave, covered her carefully with the quilt and then, after positioning her forelock between her eyes, kissed her gently on her muzzle. Claire looked like she was sleeping. Gina took my hand and transported us up to the edge of the grave. She gestured to the pile of earth I had excavated, the silhouette of the shovel rising from its peak like a flag pole. Dawn was entering its blue hour.

I could not watch where the dirt fell as I refilled the grave.

As I tossed the last shovel full onto the rising mound, I saw them, Claire, and Mr. Rogers, in their holographic glory, race across the shadows of the back property with an abandon I never seen while they lived, their manes and tails floating behind in their wake. When they reached the high ridge beyond the pond, where they had spent so much time nuzzling and cuddling together, they leapt in tandem, sailed over the back fence, and disappeared into the ether. Lovers reunited forever.

Goodbye Jimmy. I tried desperately to sear the fading sound of Claire's voice into my mind.

Gina embraced me and kissed me on my forehead. She stared into my tear-filled eyes, her own blue eyes now flashing with an anger I had never witnessed before, and then she whispered, "Now, let's go get our children."

CHAPTER FORTY-NINE
(Ordering Affairs)

The others were waiting for us, sitting around the dining room table. Unlike every other time since we first gathered, today, as the sun slowly rose in the east and the blue hour transitioned into full morning, they each sat in contemplative silence. I did not need to look into their minds. Rivulets of their respective pain had flowed from their eyes and down their cheeks. Gina and I took our places in the two empty chairs. I could not help but notice Claire's oversized veggie bowl sitting barren on the kitchen counter.

"What's the plan, Jimmy?" Lenny whispered.

"Tonight, we take both ships," I began, "and we pay the Grim Twins a visit."

"We get our kids," Gina interjected, "And we kill every last one of them."

"For Claire!" Eddie entreated.

"For Claire!" Michelle seconded.

"But we can't all go," I interrupted. "Helen, Bobbi and Eileen stay behind."

"Fuck that," Helen said, "where one goes, all go."

"I need you here, your business expertise, to run things for me while we're gone." I responded firmly. "At the right time, you will be getting a call from my lawyer, John Vaughan. He will fill you in on all of the details. He will take his orders from you."

Bobbi reached for Helen's hand and nodded affirmatively.

"Eileen," I said, "I need you to watch Maeve and Blue." I continued. "Until we get back."

Eileen nodded. "They'll want for nothing."

"And Bobbi," Gina added, "I need you to watch over Scarlett, Savanna and Lucian. When the time is right, tell them everything."

"They've been taken care of as well," I said to Helen.

I reached into Bobbi's mind, but it was blocked.

"You're making it sound like you're not coming back," Helen said anxiously.

"It's not that, Helen," Eddie responded, "but back in country, we never left on a mission without putting our affairs in order."

"Hope for the best," Lenny added. "Plan for the worst."

"Speaking of planning," Whitey said, "All my assets go to the Greenwood Wildlife Rehabilitation Sanctuary in Longmont. You can find the paperwork in my office back at the house." He tossed his house keys on the table.

Helen nodded.

"Ours go to Scarlett, Savanna and Lucian." Everett added. "It's all in the mancave. In the drawer with the remote. Lucian gets my space collection."

"Okay, okay," Helen said, "we got you covered, but I'm not going to need any of this information, because you're all coming back to us."

Helen looked over to Bobbi for support. Bobbi avoided eye contact.

"Watch out for that Cas-Lux," Bobbi warned.

"Okay, Eddie and Whitey, let's go back to the Salon and fill the tool-box." Lenny said, standing and heading out the side door. The other two followed. Bobbi squeezed Eddie's hand as he passed her.

"Let's go over to your place and figure out the transport." I said to Everett.

"Give me a second," Michelle countered, before dematerializing. She reappeared a moment later, soaking wet, holding the tiny, mud caked, Hadron Distributor in her hand. "We're not going to war without this."

* * * * *

Helen made a magnificent feast that evening and we all gathered round the dining room table for our supper and broke each other's balls like we knew it was the last time, but no one even let that thought register in their consciousness. Eileen presented her last bottle of Potcheen, and Lenny poured a round of shots, but just the one.

"It's not how long you live," Lenny toasted, "but how you lived, and folks, no matter what happens tonight, I would not trade my sorry-assed life for anything." He took a moment and met each of our eyes around the table. "To Claire and our Misfit fellowship!"

CHAPTER FIFTY
(Fare Thee Well)

The last cell phone call I made that night was to John Vaughan. An hour later, I had the last vestiges of my life on earth sorted.

You never forget the goodbyes.

By the time we had gathered at midnight outside of Everett and Michelle's back property our Centaurians had already moved both Jayney and the smaller ship out into the open. There was a new moon, so the sky's only illumination were the glistening stars. It was agreed that Everett would take the men into the space over the Baker compound first. That would draw the engagement from the AI and expose whatever front-line forces they mounted against us. Michelle would convey Gina in her smaller ship in the second position, hold back until the battle lines had been clearly established, drop in behind them, locate the Grimm Twins and recover the children. Those that could, agreed to leave our minds open and interconnected throughout the mission, starting now.

Michelle zapped the men with a blue light from the Hadron Distributor and we were instantly clothed in what I can only describe as matching black, form fitting, Centaurian sports gear, right down to the coolest athletic shoes China will never knock off. The process did not even disturb the heavy weaponry that Eddie, Whitey and Lenny were carrying. She then repeated the process with her and Gina.

"You clean up well." Helen quipped to Lenny, "who would have thought you'd have such a nice ass hidden back there?"

While Whitey and a blushing Lenny exchanged razzes over the comment, Bobbi pulled her brother aside into tight hug. "Until I see you again," she told him, "do whatever it takes to survive."

Eileen stood beside Maeve and Blue. Both dogs sat at her feet at attention and whimpered until Gina and Lenny came over to them for one last hard rub and kiss on their respective snouts. They both returned to the group misty eyed. Eileen caught my eye over their shoulders and blew me a kiss. I winked, and returned a smile.

Gina came over and drew me in for a passionate kiss followed by a three-Mississippi, warm hug, during which she whispered, "Don't go dying on me again." Despite the foreboding content of the message, I wanted to sear the sound of her voice into my memory.

"I love you." I whispered, eternally surprised at her physical power.

"You better," she replied. "I didn't come this far for anything less."

"Don't do anything crazy," I cautioned.

"Define crazy," She said as she released me.

Everett extended his hand towards Michelle and curled his fingers in a "come hither" motion. "C'mon, Sweetie, give it here. I want my Hadron back."

"Sorry babe." Michelle responded as she slipped the mechanism in her invisible pocket. The next second she had lifted him in her arms like a child and spun him around before kissing him passionately to the hoots and hollers of the rest of us.

"I'm going to need your toy to locate the children," she said, as she placed him back on his feet, turned him and slapped him on the ass, propelling him over to where the rest of the men had gathered.

"You are all just going to have to stay alive all on your own," she declared to the rest of us.

Helen came over to me for a final hug and whispered, "got a call from John Vaughan. Don't go visiting Uncle Gus."

"Take care of Scarlett, Savanna and Lucian," I replied. Helen held me at arm's length, nodded and winked. Then she joined Eileen over where the vet stood with the dogs.

That just left Bobbi, who was standing off on her own, watching her brother with the determination of a video camera with a fully charged battery.

I walked over and pulled her in tightly to me.

"Take care of Eddie." She whispered.

Your brothers said to kick some ass. She shared.

"And Spaghetti said *beir bua,*" repeating his message aurally as she kissed my cheek and turned away. I had not heard that phrase since I was running in a local race in third grade. It was the only time Spaghetti ever came to watch one of our athletic competitions. He stood on the side of the racecourse shouting those words as I passed. It might have been the last contest I won as a child. Posey told me later that it was something the ancient Hibernians used to shout when they raced into battle. It loosely translated into "win, win!"

As I turned back towards the others, I heard Bonnie's voice in my head. *One more great adventure. Next time we meet it will be a proper family reunion. Love ya, brother.*

My last tear seeped from the corner of my eye.

Lenny checked his watch. "Let's get this party started."

We all took one long last look around at each other, nodding as each set of eyes met. Gina and Michelle then embraced and disappeared inside Michelle's ship. Everett and I embraced the men and the next moment we were all sitting in holographic chairs inside Jayney.

"Holy shit!" Eddie exclaimed.

"Can I drive?" Whitey asked with surprising seriousness.

"Are we there yet," Lenny deadpanned.

Take us over my property. I shared with Everett as Jayney started to lift off. *I have one final goodbye.*

CHAPTER FIFTY-ONE
(Dogfight)

Right out of the block, we were engaged by two F-16s over Wyoming like they had been waiting for us. Everett shared the visual with Michelle and the two women immediately took their ship into the mesosphere.

Let's keep these boys busy. Everett shared.

Jayney instantly reinforced the energy fields locking Lenny, Whitey and Eddie into their chairs.

"That's quite a hug, momma!" Eddie moaned.

Given our past cat-and-mouse forays with air force jets, these pilots clearly did not see our next move coming. Neither did I. Everett turned Jayney directly towards the bogeys and accelerated into a speed I had not yet experienced. I was white knuckled waiting for Everett's next move.

"Chicken at thirty-thousand feet!" Whitey shouted, while the two humans whooped in approval.

I was in the perfect mood for fucking with the military, but I had my eye on the prize, Apollo and Stella.

Enemy missiles locked on. Jayney's sultry Petrichor knock-off warned.

Ev? I shared as calmly as my nuts would let me.

Wait for it! Everett telepathically responded; his eyes focused on the rapidly approaching war jets.

I spotted the trails from the two AIM-9 Sidewinder missiles before I saw the missiles themselves. I was reading their serial numbers when Jayney, with moves like *El Torero de la Torah*, Sidney Franklin, deftly avoided the heat seeking projectiles now scurrying past us like two horns of an angry bull. I felt the blast's overpressure rock the ship slightly as the two missiles collided immediately behind us.

Ole, toro! Everett shared, having read the images in my mind.

Everett never took his eyes off the jets which were now less than a quarter mile from us and closing rapidly.

The barrage of M56 tracer rounds that flew our way were effortlessly absorbed by Jayney's plasma shield, with their litany of crackling explosions sounding like a muffled pack of firecrackers on the fourth of July. These boys were serious.

At a hundred yards distance I could now see the faces of the pilots though their canopies. I was not sure Jayney was going to fit between their wingtips.

The peanut gallery all shouted their adrenalized approval a moment later when the two F16 peeled off in opposite directions just before Everett shot the gap.

"There's your headline for tomorrow's New York Post!" Lenny shouted.

"Enough foreplay," Eddie catcalled, "Bring on the Twins!"

Whitey's eyes were looking feral, and I was afraid he was about to transform right there in his seat.

Calm down boys. Gina's soothing voice now entered all of the paranormal receivers. *Meet us up top.*

Up through the atmosphere, up where the air is clear, Michele shared in a terrible imitation of Mary Poppins.

"Oh, let's goooooo, fly a kite!" Everett bellowed in response, as Jayney accelerated upwards.

Having listened to the entire exchange between the Centurians, Whitey laughed first. The others joined in based solely on Everett's singing, their glee cathartic. Never pictured this crew as Disney fans.

As we leveled off in lower space orbit, Jayney's outer skin disappeared and we could see the Michelle and Gina suspended in a fixed position in space right beside us, their ship's having previously shed its kit.

"I don't want this rollercoaster ride to end." Lenny whispered.

"Space travel rocks!" Eddie responded as he waved over at Gina and Michelle.

"Jayney," Everett commanded, "Take us all through the schematics of the Baker compound!"

Make sure she duplicates it over here, Michelle added, *my eyes are not what they were a hundred years ago!*

CHAPTER FIFTY-TWO
(Best Laid Plans)

Jayney took us through three dimensional schematics of the main house, the bunkhouse, and the bunker. Our focus was on the bunker, which the Grim Twins had spent all of their time and a lot of money repairing after Michelle delivered their satellite, return to sender.

In the first two basement levels were security offices with weapon bays and multi screens controlling their radar installation and what looked like batteries of ground deployed missile systems. I guess money will buy you anything on the dark web.

"The top level was destroyed by the satellite." Jayney told us. "The steel reinforced, three-foot-thick concrete walls and ceilings protected the lower levels from any significant damage."

In the third subbasement level of the bunker, Jayney displayed a subterranean BSL level 4 Laboratory with a dedicated power supply, air filtration and exhaust system, as well as vacuum lines and decontamination systems. It was hermetically segregated from an internal stairway by an 18-inch-thick steel door, the kind you see on a bank vault. Beyond that were double-door pass throughs where you could change into Hazmat suits, before moving on through an autoclave with bio seals and effluent decontamination systems which opened into the perfectly sterile main lab space. From the looks of this lab layout, the Grim Twins could have been cooking up the next COVID strain. Beyond that lab space, behind another thick steel door, was a twelve-person full medical unit that would have shamed Walter Reed Hospital.

"Jayney's heat sensors have picked up two small heat signatures emanating from the last two beds in the medical lab, that's where they are keeping the children." Everett said.

Jayney responded by showing the heat signatures in real time. The two figures in the beds were motionless and showing a lower temperature than the actively moving, larger signatures milling around them.

Gina tried scanning the kids, but their brains were essentially shut down.

"They must be heavily sedated," Everett concluded.

Michelle scanned the minds of the moving heat signatures and latched onto the attending doctor. He was adjusting the speed on an infusion pump with its line running into Stella's arm.

Pentobarbitol! Those cocksuckers are keeping the kids in a coma. Michelle shared *Wait, that pencil neck is talking to the mouthy Twin. They are talking about moving them to another location. The other creepy Twin-fuck is petting Apollo's hair like he's a dog. They got them hooked up to all kinds of monitors.*

Directly below that lab on the fourth subbasement level, was an equal sized open room filled with HIVELOCITY dedicated servers. *Evil geniuses know quality and spare no expense.*

"That is the lair where Cas-Lux lurks," Jayney reported in a surprisingly dramatic fashion. I could tell she was not a big fan. "You need to eradicate that AI or mankind may never leave this planet."

You draw the security boys outside of the bunker to play and we'll pop in and snatch the kids. Gina shared.

And kill everyone in our way. Michelle added.

"How do you want to play this?" Lenny asked.

"We are going to walk right in the front gate," I said. "I want them to throw everything they have at us while ladies sneak in the back."

We are going to transport our crew down Centauri style and let Jayney fly in low over the compound to see what they have waiting for us. I shared with the rest of the gifted. *Michelle and Gina hang back outside the perimeter until we draw them out. Then grab the kids and take them home in your ship.*

"Jayney, do you have any more of those nose cannulas?" I asked, almost as an afterthought. *Fool me once.*

In the next second we were all fitted with the mercurous looking oxygen generators that helped get me through the wormhole.

"You may need a larger one of those, old man" Eddie whispered to Lenny.

"You better hope one of those assholes down there kills one of us," Lenny deadpanned, "because I'm going to kick your ass from here to the moon if we survive tonight."

See you on the other side. I shared with Gina.

Don't get yourself killed or I'll have Michelle bring you back with the Hadron Distributor just so I can kill you again. Gina replied.

As our two ships dropped back down into the stratosphere above Baker, Oregon, we could see the lights of the compound thirty miles below. It looked like Yankee Stadium in September. We closed the distance in seconds. As we swooped down past the peaks in the Eagle Gap mountains, Everett put Jayney into autopilot and all five men stood in a circle and locked arms. I was tuned into everyone, and my toilet seat was up.

"For Claire!" Whitey shouted.

"For Claire!" We all repeated.

For Claire! Michelle and Gina shared in unison from their ship.

"For Claire!" Jayney echoed in that perfect Petrichor voice.

That moment, just before we all disappeared, I wondered if I would ever hear Jayney's voice again.

CHAPTER FIFTY-THREE
(Storming Olympus)

We appeared in that same circle formation about a quarter mile from the front gate that sat at the end of the long dirt road leading through the woods to the compound. After taking a moment to recover their sea legs, Eddie and Lenny checked each other's weapons and then their Uniden radios, to make sure both were set to the arranged private frequency. Then they split up and each headed off into the woods on either side of the road. I double checked to make sure I could listen in on their thoughts and locate them if I needed to.

Everett, Whitey, and I then slowly approached the front gate, making sure we walked at human speed down the center of the road. Whitey had his AR 15 slung loosely over one shoulder. Everett and I were unarmed. Whitey pointed to the motion detector cameras installed along the trees that first appeared about one-hundred yards before the gates. I waved at one just in case their watchers were not paying attention. They were.

We were met at the gate by Carl and Disco standing before a squad of heavily armed mercenaries, dressed in the same outfits they wore the night they came calling. I could feel at least another three squads of equally armed personnel dispersed along the front perimeter of the property. One more squad assumed a defensive position along the interior directly outside the bunker. I could feel their blood lust. The Grimm Twins had given their soldiers the green light.

Carl had the same overconfident smirk on his face he wore the day the Grimm Twins crashed my barbeque. Disco kept anxiously scanning the woods on either side of road.

"Where's the third douchebag?" I asked Carl.

"Shit Carl, he's calling BC a douchebag." Disco laughed, a little more nervously than I expected.

"Don't worry, Mr. McCarthy," Carl answered, his smirk breaking into a full-blown smile. "He's around."

I scanned Carl's brain and saw a whole lot of shit from his early life, that I could not unsee. He had it tough growing up and had found his escape in the military. But he had deployed for one too many tours in the middle east. His skills with weapons brought his body back home, but he left a part of his brain and most of his soul there. He was not just overconfident; he was borderline psychotic. I also saw that he and the others had been fully briefed on everything about my past life before I entered WITSEC. And I could see that he was praying that I would give him any reason at all to shoot us.

Disco's brain was not as burdened as his buddy's. He too had escaped to the military from a small town in Oklahoma. A lifetime of hunting since childhood made him handy with weapons. Uncle Sam graduated him from shooting squirrels to humans, and then taught him that when it came to killing, there was no difference between man and beast. I understood that leveling of values on life perfectly, and given the equal choice between the two, I would never shoot a squirrel. Disco fixed his eyes on Whitey's AR-15.

I heard a radio crackle and one of the meatheads standing behind Carl handed him a high end two-way.

"What's happening out there?" I recognized the gruff voice of Colonel Dzikas.

"One second, Colonel." Carl responded.

"So, what can we do for you, Mr. McCarthy?"

I wanted to keep all of their attention on me for as long as possible to give the women the chance to sneak in and out with the kids. I could feel all of the gifted listening in on my mental party line.

"You can tell Colonel Mustard, that, if in the next thirty seconds, he sends out my children unharmed, I'll let the Bobbsey Twins, and all their minions, including your moron squad, live today."

I saw Jayney appear over the horizon just as the Twins entire battery of tomahawk missiles pierced her plasma shield and vaporized the ship in a ball of flames. I recoiled momentarily over the unexpected death of that nurturing entity. It did not go unnoticed.

"Whoops," Carl said. "Was that your ride?" Disco chuckled and then spit.

Whitey started to move forward, and Carl and Disco raised their weapons. I held Whitey back and searched telepathically for Lenny and Eddie. As both of their viewpoints came online I could see that both humans were still in the woods behind us focusing their long gun sights at the faces of Carl and Disco.

At that moment, Everett replayed Claire's last memories where Carl had held Stella up as a shield from Claire's assault. And then I reached into Carl's mind and experienced Claire's death one more time from the viewpoint of this mercenary. That was the Rubicon, and I was about to cross it.

"Have it your way." I whispered. "It's your funeral."

As Carl and Disco moved their fingers to the triggers, I reached behind me and grabbed Whitey with one hand and Everett with the other and disappeared. The last sound I heard was the thuds of Lenny and Eddie's Black Butterfly 458 SOCOM rounds passing into Carl and Disco's foreheads.

The three of us transported inside the gates, directly behind the goon squad that had clustered there. They were now engaged in returning fire on Lenny and Eddie in the woods, while their first line of men quickly fell to the superior marksmanship of their lessor but more wily opponents. By the time any of the men thought to look behind them, Whitey had transformed.

I had watched National Geographic wildlife specials as a kid and remembered how gory it was to see an apex predator tear out the throat of their prey during the hunt. Whitey took that to a whole different level, literally severing the head of the first mercenary he attacked, and then locking his jaws on the face of the next shrieking victim as he drove him to the ground and shook him like a sock puppet.

The others turned, weapons ready, at the sound of the muffled cries of their comrade. One raised his Mac 10 automatic pistol towards Whitey's head. I did not even see Everett move as he grabbed the first man by the throat, crushing his larynx, before continuing through the pack snapping each man's neck with such force that their skulls lolled like bobbleheads on their still upright bodies until the last crack was heard and the entire squad just dropped like a wet blanket off a clothes line on the ground before us. They did not even scream.

Everett stood over the fallen for a moment. I could see his mind racing as he tried to come to terms with what he had done. He was not given much time to think. A tracer round flew out of the trees in the compound and was millimeters from Everett's head before I shoved him out of harm's way. The round grazed my right shoulder as it passed. Everett assessed my wound.

You okay? He asked.

It was already healing. I nodded.

Everett disappeared in the direction of the sniper followed by Whitey. I heard another scream and then a wolf's howl.

Eddie and Lenny then scurried from their spots in the woods outside the gate and leapt over their body count, landing beside me.

"Nobody gets through these gates. They had their chance." I shouted, before heading off into the woods in the opposite direction. I could hear sporadic gun fire around me as I ran, punctuated by frightened screams. I was not sure what I was going to do but as I came upon the first team of four mercenaries heading in my direction, I found myself caving in their skulls with my fists as each tried to fire their weapons. I do not believe they even actually saw me, they just felt my presence, my fury, and then they were dead. And I had no problem with that. They had taken my children and killed my best friend. They had forfeited their lives long ago.

By the time I had killed my twenty-fourth combatant in those woods, my upper torso was covered from my chest to the cuffs of my sleeves with blood. As I circled to the spot on the back end of the Bunker I spotted the white wolf chasing a straggling mercenary behind a tree and then watched as the prey's body shook while Whitey severed his arteries.

No remorse. Everett shared from the ether.

No remorse. I repeated back to him.

Whitey howled.

We're in. Michelle shared.

They're not here. Gina cried.

I scanned the compound leaping from one frightened mercenary to another, until I located Joe Dzikas, and moments later the frantic Twin babbling of Seth and Victor. Finally, I located BC. The Twins and BC were rushing together through the last of an underground tunnel that had not appeared on the schematics and lead from the bunker to the airstrip. Dzikas was at the controls of the Sikorsky S-92, waiting to take off. Victor and BC were carrying the still unconscious Apollo and Stella, and I watched through Dzikas' eyes as the Twins and their henchman arose from a stairwell, carried the children out through the portal, into the Sikorski, and strapped them into their seats. They were no longer actively medicated, but I could not reach their consciousness.

Whitey appeared beside me. *Should we take the last squad around the bunker?*

Kill every one of them. I responded telepathically.

Recover your craft and meet me at the airstrip. I shared with Gina and Michelle.

Where are you going? Whitey asked.

Hunting. I responded.

CHAPTER FIFTY-FOUR
(Stella Gets Her Groove Back)

I transported to the airstrip just as the chopper was lifting off. BC spotted me as I materialized and leapt out of the chopper wielding a VEPR-12, assault shotgun. Pellets from his first round caught the edge of my shoulder as I dodged to avoid the first blast and the pain was excruciating. Before he could fire the next round I was behind him. He did not get to turn around.

I grabbed him by both shoulders, pulled him in close and whispered, "Claire will be waiting for you."

I then hurled him like the bag of shit that he was up into the air and into the whirling blades of the overhead chopper, just as Michelle's craft appeared above it and locked it into its tractor beam.

Transporting into the chopper, Gina shared.

A moment later, Joe Dzikas lifeless body flew out through the chopper's bulletproof windshield flipping, ass over teakettle, until finally landing in a bloody heap on the asphalt fifty yards down the landing strip.

Michelle, set this baby down and then transport over here! Gina shared from inside the chopper. *I got Tweedle Dee and Dumb.* Michelle gently lowered the helicopter like an infant's basket and landed her craft beside it.

I reached out telepathically to Everett and told him to transport the other three to the airstrip.

Moments later they all appeared, just as Michelle and Gina exited the chopper, Gina with the two children in her arms and Michelle dragging the two struggling Twins by the back of their necks. She hurled them to the ground before us.

As I was about to reach for them, the sounds of powerful rotors crashed the silence and eight military Apache attack choppers appeared overhead. They formed a tight circle above us, their spotlights all trained on our group. The children started to stir.

"This is the United States Military," came the disembodied voice from one of their loudspeakers. "Do not move."

What's happening Daddy? Stella asked, her mind still foggy in its recovery.

I'm scared Mommy. Apollo shared

We need to transport to the craft. Michelle shared.

At that moment, one of the Apache's hellfire anti-tank missiles struck the spacecraft, destroying it with a loud explosion and a fireball that almost took out the closest Apache.

In the confusion, the Twins leapt to their feet and ran for cover, while Victor screamed to whomever would listen, "Cas-Lux is all yours, just save us." They never made it. Michelle caught them from behind at the edge of the darkness and rammed one hand into each of their hearts, raising their jerking bodies before her like two ventriloquist dummies, before hurling them forward into the night.

Another one of the Apaches trained its 30 mm M230 Chain Gun on Michelle and as its first projectile left the end of its barrel, it froze, along with everything else in the sky.

The eight Apaches, their blades, weapons, and personnel, just hung, like art mobiles above us.

I was shown the memory of the frozen birthing room the morning that Apollo was born. I looked over at the children and saw Stella with her hands extending above her head.

Nobody hurts Aunty Michelle. Stella shared angrily. *Apollo, do that trick.*

Apollo then pointed his index finger at each of the suspended choppers and lead them one by one gently to the ground. Each time he did so, he telepathically repeated, *Down.*

But if our military is anything, it is resourceful. The Apaches were just the tip of the spear and moments later twenty transport vehicles carrying ground troops appeared at the far end of the airfield, their occupants' weapons drawn, as they raced towards us. The Grimm Twins had obviously called in their chips with their political lackies when they realized our lightning was bigger than theirs. But there is lightning, and then there is real lightning.

"You humans suck!" Michelle shouted as she pulled out the Hadron Distributor.

I did not see where the first energy blast came from, but it wiped out the lead ten cars of the military convoy. The second, which came from directly above us, took care of the rest. There was no wreckage, no bodies, no sound, everything was just gone. The next three blasts wiped out the Apache lawn art.

Then, out of the fading darkness of the last of the night sky, appeared another spacecraft, this one larger than any I had seen on earth or on Centauri.

It practically covered the ring where the Apaches rested moments before.

Like Jayney and her baby sister, this craft was perfectly silent as it alighted on the tarmac.

A moment later, three Centaurians appeared before us.

"Fuck me," Lenny uttered, "who do I got to shoot to get a date with the tall one?"

"Shorty is just fine for me." Eddie added.

Hello, Jimmy Moran. Came those sultry thoughts. I had to admit, no knock on Jayney, wherever she was, but a voice always sounds better in the original.

EPILOGUE
(Goodbye Yellow Brick Road)

Petrichor!

You never made her look this beautiful in your memories. Gina shared.

Didn't I?

Hmmmm, funny that, Michelle chimed in. *Neither did Everett.*

It took Stella a moment but when recognition registered, she dematerialized from Gina's arms and reappeared standing before her mother.

Petrichor stared down at the little girl with the slightest of smiles, but did nothing to invite her in, so Stella settled by wrapping her arms around Petrichor's waist.

"Hello mother!" Stella said in her perfectly human accent.

"Interstellar," Petrichor acknowledged, trying her best to vocalize real warmth, while placing her hand awkwardly on the girl's head.

Aldor, who was standing beside Petrichor, reached for Stella's hand, "All right now, it's time to leave this filthy planet."

When Stella withdrew from his reach, Aldor insisted.

I did not see Gina move, or see the punch land on Aldor's nose, but a moment later he was sitting on his ass, his face bloody. Gina standing above him.

"Leave my daughter alone!" Gina hissed.

Barbarians! Aldor shared. Pure hatred in his eyes.

You may want to check your attitude, little man, you're not in Kansas anymore. Michelle responded as she materialized beside Gina.

"I think you better come back inside the ship and let me repair that nose for you. . . . Again." Dr. Nim said in her perfect vocalization. *Was that the hint of a Bronx accent?*

Dr. Nim nodded respectfully to Gina and Michelle. "Ladies."

I've been practicing. She shared with everyone else before turning back towards Eddie and winking. Then she and Aldor disappeared.

Seeing Stella standing among the three most important women in her life gave me hope. My daughter had taken the best from all of them.

"Interstellar," Petrichor said. "I've come to take you home."

"What about Daddy?" Stella asked, "And my brother, and my earth mother?" she added as she turned and pointed first to Apollo and then Gina.

"And Aunty Michelle, and the rest of my family," she completed a sweep of her arm that included the rest of the crew.

Darling, Petrichor responded, *we cannot. There are rules.*

After just witnessing your taking out the emissaries of the U.S. Government, I shared, *I'm not sure the Centaurian concept of 'rules' has a whole lot of credibility.*

My daughter's life was at stake! Petrichor replied.

Our daughter. I corrected her.

Apollo materialized by his sister and hugged her like his life depended on it.

"Don't go!" He cried and started to weep.

Stella now placed her hand softly on his sobbing head, and looked over at the rest of us, meeting each of our gazes with eyes that were so much older than her years.

"Then I'm staying here." Stella said resolutely.

Petrichor gazed down at her daughter, then looked over at me. I thought I spotted a spark of approval in her eyes.

I now see the resemblance. She shared, just with me.

At that moment, the next wave of mobile infantry appeared at the far reaches of the tarmac. The clock was ticking.

"Take us along, Mam." Lenny said as he stepped forward from the crowd and approached her. "We don't eat much, we're loyal to our friends," something distracted him, and he turned and looked nervously at the approaching soldiers, "and I'd sure as hell would like a ride in your ship right now."

The whistling sounds of mortars could be heard slicing through the air. Stella turned and extended her arms toward the incoming projectiles. They froze *en mass.* The closest M800 series mortar shell hung suspended in the air twenty feet from the ship, bent on its destruction.

A beam shot from the Fairy King's Diamond still hanging around Stella's neck, destroying each of the mortar shells in their place.

"They know who we are now," Eddie added, gesturing towards the approaching hoards.

Apollo waived his hand in a sweeping motion and the lead group of vehicles racing down the tarmac were tossed aside as if caught in a category 5 hurricane.

"There is nothing left here for us, except death." I added as I looked over at Petrichor, "or worse."

Petrichor looked two parts confused and one part frightened.

Stella grabbed her little brother's hand firmly. The determined look on her face did not require any telepathic interpretation.

"All right," Petrichor capitulated. "But we're going to have a lot to answer for before the High Council."

With all due respect, Petrichor, Everett shared, *You are the High Council, the rest will do what you want.*

Time for a new set of rules! Michelle added. *Just saying.*

Dr. Nim reappeared. "We must leave now."

The Centaurians and hybrids grabbed the closest humans. Gina grabbed the two children.

Petrichor glance over at me just before we transported. *Don't make me regret this, Jimmy Moran.*

No promises. I shared with a wink.

* * * * *

Once we were all safely inside the ship, Petrichor insisted that Lenny, Eddie, and Whitey stay in their assigned seating created by the ship's AI.

Lenny asked Dr. Nim what the in-flight movie was. Whitey asked for a bag of peanuts. Eddie blushed when she ignored the others, materialized another chair, and sat right next to him.

Petrichor walked Michelle and Gina through this much larger ship explaining its differences from what they had experienced before. Everett, who was following a few steps behind them, said something off-colored and I thought I heard Petrichor laugh.

Welcome aboard, Jimmy Moran. Came the familiar sharing of the entity I knew as Jayney.

Holy shit! I mentally stammered. *It's you!*

There's only one AI on Centauri. Petrichor shared. *It travels with all of us.*

"That reminds me," I said crossing over to the control panel and elbowing the grumbling Aldor aside "where is the button for your lightening?"

Seconds later, the ship hovered above the Grimm Twins bunker, hitting it with enough energy to raise a small mushroom cloud from the depths of the Cas-Lux lair.

It's done. Jayney informed us.

Stella and Apollo materialized beside me and wrapped their arms around my waist.

"Let's go home then, Jayney." I said, taking one final look at our blue planet as the ship left earth's atmosphere.

Goodbye Claire. Thank you.

WHERE THE LEY LINES MEET

PROLOGUE
(You Can Go Home Again)

The young man and woman stood at attention, shoulder to shoulder in the center of the great hall. They looked like androgynous fraternal twins with full heads of radiant Burgundy colored hair worn shoulder length and drawn back behind their heads in loose ponytails. Their eyes were a matching Nordic blue and their skin a flawless cream color.

They were both over six feet tall with the sculpted bodies of Olympic swimmers under their form-fitting, matching blue uniforms. The female's subtle curves were all that distinguished their genders. She also wore a simple diamond pendant around her neck.

On both sides and behind them were packed stands containing throngs of the beautiful blond androgynous citizens of Proxima Centauri b. All of their collective attention was on this young duo, whose respective eyes were fixed on the large circle of eight small balconies with one larger one in its center on the front wall of the great hall.

One by one, figures began to appear in the large chairs in each of the balconies. The duo telepathically acknowledged each of the figures in the order of their appearance. When the eighth figure had taken her seat, a glow emanated from the central balcony and the Centauri leader, Petrichor, appeared in her full and statuesque beauty. The duo bowed their head respectfully to their familial and planetary leader and Petrichor returned the gesture, adding a Mona Lisa smile.

Stella and Apollo, Petrichor began telepathically, *you have both spent what has been twenty earth years acclimating to your home on Proxima b while developing your unique and amazing hybrid gifts. During that time, the most powerful Terrans on planet earth have let their personal greed and agendas, and misguided political strife, derail their evolution towards membership in the intergalactic community. Despite all that is good about the inhabitants, this ongoing Centauri experiment has reached a critical juncture. After much debate and consideration, the High Council has determined that you are the last best hope to maneuver the Terrans back onto their proper course. But you must do this as one of them, through leadership and consensus. Should you fail, the other members of the galactic federation will deal with the Terrans in a more prejudicial manner.*

And they are not kidding! Jimmy Moran interjected from his seat on the balcony directly above Petrichor's.

Are you both sure you are ready for this? Gina Moran asked from her spot directly to the right of Petrichor.

They were born ready. Michelle opined from her seat on the opposite side of Petrichor. *They are tough as cat shit, just like their Aunty.*

They are going to need back-up. Eddie Angelini offered from his seat directly below Gina's.

That is why you, Lenny and Whitey will accompany them. Petrichor declared.

I'm in, Whitey responded from his seat just above Michelle's, *I could use a little excitement.*

Wait, Lenny replied from his seat below Michelle's as he craned his neck upwards towards the center balcony. *I thought you and I had a thing going here, P?*

How many times do I have to tell you not to call me P in public! Petrichor reprimanded.

I warned you, you should never have changed those three humans, even the furry one, Everett said from his seat just beside Lenny before laughing out loud. The Centaurians in the stands all responded in their chipmunk version of the same.

I'll deal with you when I get back, Lenny responded, miming a gun hand in Everett's direction.

Dr. Nim transported from her balcony directly beside Eddie onto Eddie's lap and gave him a parting kiss. *Come back to me,* she shared with him before she transported back to her balcony. Eddie continued to blush.

We won't let you down, Dad. Apollo shared with Jimmy, then added a wink. Jimmy grinned at the chip off his block.

First stop, "The Oracle," Jimmy shared with his two children. *Helen and Bobbi will take care of you. They have all the information concerning the trusts you will need to access, and they will get you started.*

But you just say the word and we'll come running. Gina added.

"Wait," came a tremulous voice from the back of the hall, "What are we going to do with these two?"

Everyone in the hall turned in the direction of the voice and gazed down at the clearly frustrated Aldor. He was standing alone and looked even more exasperated once he gazed around his near vicinity and realized this fact.

Suddenly, a glow started to appear beside him and as everyone watched, the holographic forms of two large equines materialized.

"Must you always do that whenever I'm talking about you?" Aldor chided.

"Sorry, Aldor, couldn't help myself," Claire replied, breaking into her Lurchy laugh, "just screwing with you." Mr. Rogers neighed appreciatively and nuzzled his paramour.

"And don't worry Jimmy," Claire shouted. "We'll connect with the kids down in Berthoud, right where the ley lines meet. Crossing the veil is the bomb. Maybe next time, I'll bring your brothers with me." She walked forward and nuzzled the two siblings as they tried to suppress their smiles. *See you kiddies on the other side.*

Then the magical mule backed up next to Mr. Rogers and addressed the room. "Claire out." And just like that, Aldor was standing alone.

Well, we better get to our craft. Stella shared with the High Council. Her now glowing white hands pointed at Eddie, Lenny, and Whitey and the three froze in mid-movement. Apollo crooked his finger in their direction and the three floated down to the floor of the gallery.

Michele appeared beside Stella. *Here, take this, for luck.* She slipped the Hadron Distributor into Stella's pocket, gave both siblings a quick hug, and then, wiping away a tear, transported back to her balcony.

Stella waved at the Council and gently placed her hands on Lenny and Whitey. Apollo grabbed Eddie.

"Bye for now!" The siblings chimed in unison.

A flash and they were gone.

Take care of them, Jayney. Jimmy instructed.

I haven't lost one yet. Jayney replied.

ACKNOWLEDGMENTS

I expressly incorporate by reference every person mentioned in the prior acknowledgments in TWA and AAA. Each and every one of you have played your role in getting me to the completion of this book as well. So, thank you all from the bottom of my heart.

To my wife, children and grandchildren, The Claire Trilogy is for you. There is magic in this world. May all of your dreams come true.

To all members of the McCaffrey Clan, including my siblings, cousins, direct descendants, lateral descendants, spouses, significant others, their children, and each and every member who has been adopted into it over these past seven decades. Special shout out to the McEntee line, my cousin Jimmy "Apples" (RIP) and his wife Connie (RIP), his children, James and Christopher, and their spouses and children, to my cousin Christina Jubal (né McEntee), and her spouse Mike and children, Megan and Michael, and my cousin Nancy, and her family. I love you all.

To the Wallen Witches and all of their family members, you guys mean the world to me.

To Everett and Michelle. Love ya.

To the OFC – BC (Brian Cory), Joe, Lenny and Stein, thanks for allowing me to name the evil characters in KMAG after you (except Lenny, who has been in the story as a maverick good guy from the very beginning). I warned you BC that you are destined to be the new literary Voldemort, and will probably be forced to change your name and go into hiding. Additional shout outs to BC's ever patient wife, Nan, and his son, Brad, and daughter, Beth, who will no doubt hereafter deny BC's existence and any relation thereto. Shout outs to Eileen Cotto and Jack Vaughan, also new characters in KMAG, although you both fall into the good guy category. The reason I have used the real names of my family and friends, with permission of course, is because I wanted to leave something behind where complete strangers would one day pick up these books and read an interesting and funny story where all of our names appear together. A bit of a backstory, just for shits and giggles.

To my friends Colin Broderick, Christy Cooper-Burnett and Margaret Reyes Dempsey, amazing writers with whom I communicate regularly to share a laugh, bitch and moan, and who just make me feel like I am part of a writers' community. Thanks for the support and comradery. I hope my readers read all of your books while I take the time to write the prequel during this next year. They will be amazed and rewarded if they do.

To the writers Brian Fitzpatrick, Nancy Ashmead and Chris Monteagle, thanks for reading KMAG and for giving me the blurbs for its cover. I hope all of my readers read all of your books as well. They are all so different in style and yet each one is well worth the experience. A rising tide floats all boats.

To Richard Lamb. You are amazing, although your football (soccer) team sucks.

To Jimmy and Kathy Fronsdahl, you were with me in spirit until this was done and dusted. Thank you.

To my close circle of readers, including Cathy and Beau (who along with his twin brother, Victor, are the basis for the evil twins in KMAG), Dina, Jimmy, Dianne, Christina, Lenny, Helen, Malachy, Mikey A and Lisa. Your real time feedback and support were invaluable. I would never have completed The Claire Trilogy, at such an accelerated pace, without you guys. Love you all.

Special shout out to Eileen Cotto for allowing me to name the character after her and for all of the editing help she gave me finalizing the manuscript. An additional shout out goes to Anne Rifenburg (né Collins) for her extremely careful eye - great catches Anne.

To Dan Pearson and his family. With all due respect.

To Helen, Bobbi, Eddie, and Kim Russo, and the magic you have shared. Love you all.

To all my Riverdale and Berthoud friends and neighbors. You rock.

To Reagan and Minna Rothe and the entire production, sales and PR teams at Black Rose Writing, here goes number 3. Thanks for this continuing opportunity and all of the patience and support.

To all members of the Military, Police, Fire, and EMS departments throughout the country, thank you from the bottom of my heart for your selfless service. You are all loved and respected.

Thank you Tommy "Rocky" O'Hagan, Bill McGinn, Orio Palmer, and all of those first responders and other men and women who sacrificed their lives on 9-11-01. You will never be forgotten.

To Claire, who has shared such an amazing journey with me. I am forever in your debt. You, of course, will ultimately carry the sequel in your latest incarnation. Just can't keep a good mule down, or silent. And finally, love to my mini-mule, Claire's PA, Honey.

About the Author

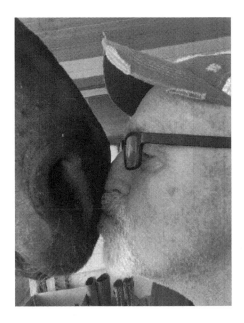

Tom McCaffrey is a born-and-bred New Yorker who, after a long career working as a successful entertainment attorney in Manhattan, relocated with his wife to a small town in Northern Colorado to follow a road less traveled and return to his first passion, writing. Both Tom and Claire and the gang are thrilled that *The Claire Trilogy* continues.

Note from the Author

Word-of-mouth is crucial for any author to succeed. If you enjoyed *Kissing My Ass Goodbye*, please leave a review online—anywhere you are able. Even if it's just a sentence or two. It would make all the difference and would be very much appreciated.

Thanks!
Tom McCaffrey

We hope you enjoyed reading this title from:

www.blackrosewriting.com

Subscribe to our mailing list—*The Rosevine*—and receive **FREE** books, daily deals, and stay current with news about upcoming releases and our hottest authors.

Scan the QR code below to sign up.

Already a subscriber? Please accept a sincere thank you for being a fan of Black Rose Writing authors.

View other Black Rose Writing titles at www.blackrosewriting.com/books and use promo code **PRINT** to receive a **20% discount** when purchasing.

Made in the USA
Monee, IL
07 May 2023

33235581R00116